The most beautiful horse in the world. . . .

Sterling began to trot around the little ring. She kept her eye on Christina as she threw her slender front legs before her in a beautifully smooth extension. The mare nearly floated, her perfect neck arched, her neat black hooves hardly touching the ground. She seemed to be showing off for Christina, who watched delightedly.

"Is this the horse?"

Christina turned and saw her mother. She nodded, beaming happily. "Isn't she gorgeous? Just look at that extended trot."

Ashleigh and Christina watched as the mare stopped, spun on her haunch, and began to canter gracefully around in the other direction. Christina sighed. She had never wanted something so badly in her life. And it didn't look like she would ever be able to have it.

Collect all the books in the Thoroughbred series

Collect all the books in the Ashleigh series

coming soon*

THOROUGHBRED

THE HORSE OF HER DREAMS

CREATED BY
JOANNA CAMPBELL

WRITTEN BY
ALLISON ESTES

HarperPaperbacks
A Division of HarperCollins*Publishers*

HarperPaperbacks

A Division of HarperCollins*Publishers*
10 East 53rd Street, New York, N.Y. 10022-5299

Copyright © 1998 by Daniel Weiss Associates, Inc. and Joanna Campbell

ISBN 0-06-106797-0

HarperCollins®, 📕®, and HarperPaperbacks™ are trademarks of HarperCollins*Publishers* Inc.

Cover art: © 1998 Daniel Weiss Associates, Inc.

First printing: February 1998

Printed in the United States of America

Visit HarperPaperbacks on the World Wide Web at
http://www.harpercollins.com

❖ 10 9 8 7

I wish to acknowledge the following people:
Maureen Mack, for patiently and thoroughly answering
questions on her lunch break every Saturday;

Bob Curran of Thoroughbred Racing Communications,
Thoroughbred racing's national media-relations office, for
graciously lending me his time and resources;

Fran Labelle, media information coordinator for
Aqueduct and Belmont, for his generosity in
taking me and my daughter on a tour of Belmont
Race Track at six o'clock in the morning.

For more information on
Thoroughbred racing, contact:

Thoroughbred Racing Communications, Inc.
40 East 52 Street
New York, NY 10022
(212) 371–5910 (phone)
(212) 371–5917 (fax)

TWELVE-YEAR-OLD CHRISTINA REESE LEANED AGAINST THE fence surrounding the oval training track at White- brook Farm. Her cheeks were cold in the early morn- ing air, but the March sun felt warm on her back. It glinted off her strawberry blond hair and highlighted the reddish coat of the horse trotting down the far side of the track.

Christina pulled the sleeves of her jacket over her fingers, rested her chin on her folded arms, and watched her breath steam out in the chilly air. Far down the track she could see tiny, twin puffs of steam come from the colt's nostrils as he rounded the turn and headed toward her. He tossed his head, impatient at being held to a brisk trot. Let me run, he seemed to be saying. Christina felt as impatient as the colt. She just wasn't that interested in watching a workout, no matter how impressive the horse. She would rather be grooming her pony, getting him ready for her jump lesson.

January and February had been unusually cold and snowy for Kentucky, but March had come like a sunny apology for the harsh winter. Today the ground would be soft enough to jump outside, and Christina could hardly wait for ten o'clock so she could go down the road to Gardener Farm for her riding lesson, but she had promised her mother she would watch this horse's workout.

Christina studied the beautiful colt as he trotted past. His name was Wonder's Legacy, and his shiny, chestnut coat gleamed over his firm muscles and excellent bones. Like his dam, Wonder, he had four white stockings and a broad white blaze on his handsome face, but Wonder had been small and fine-boned. Legacy was big for a just-turned-two-year-old, and the look of fierce determination in his eyes spoke for his future as a racehorse.

"What do you think? Our boy's looking good, isn't he?"

Christina turned and saw the head trainer of Whitebrook Farm, Ian McLean. Christina nodded in agreement. "He looks great," she said.

"That colt's going to be Whitebrook's next champion for sure," Ian said matter-of-factly. He leaned against the rail next to Christina.

Christina's parents, Ashleigh Griffen and Michael

2

Reese, were the owners of Whitebrook Farm. Together with Ian McLean, they had worked for the last several years to make Whitebrook Farm a superior Thoroughbred breeding and training facility. The farm had become well known for producing winning animals, not just around Lexington, but all over the country.

There was a sudden burst of hoofbeats on the track and the horse was off. "Look at him go!" Ian said, grasping Christina's arm in his enthusiasm. "Just look at him stretch! He loves it! That's a fine colt right there—he's quality through and through, just like his dam," Ian added, giving Christina a knowing wink.

Ian was talking about her mother's first horse, Wonder. Ashleigh's Wonder had been a Kentucky Derby winner and many-time champion in her younger days. Now she was old and hollow-backed, but her coat still gleamed and the look of steady courage in her large brown eyes had never faltered. Wonder's racing and breeding days were over, but she had thrown many champion colts and fillies.

Christina had grown up playing in the paddocks and barn aisles of Whitebrook, surrounded by foals who grew up to become famous racehorses. One of her earliest memories was of sitting upon Wonder's back, her mother encouraging her to pet the mare's soft coat. But unlike her mother, who had tirelessly tended Wonder when she was a sickly foal and brought her along until her racing days, Christina just didn't have the same passion for racehorses. She loved horses and she loved living at Whitebrook, but she couldn't seem to get excited about watching a horse gallop around a dirt track. Christina loved to jump.

Wonder's Legacy flashed past her then, a look of keen intensity on his face. The clocker punched the button on top of his stopwatch with a triumphant gesture and the heads of all the onlookers turned. All except for Christina.

Christina's eyes were no longer on the stellar colt in the training oval. Instead her gaze had drifted upward, to a hillside beyond one of the pastures. She hugged the top rail of the fence, looking with interest at a good-sized tree that had come down in an ice storm that winter. She was thinking that if she could get up there later and clear away some of the branches and debris, the trunk of the fallen tree would make a perfect jump.

"Did you see that?" Anna Simms, Legacy's sixteen-year-old exercise rider, had trotted over to Christina on the pretty colt. She pulled her goggles off and beamed at Christina, her brown eyes shining with delight. "He was flying down that last furlong and I was just sitting there. He's got more in him—I can feel it!" Legacy pranced in place, obviously proud of himself. Anna's face glowed from the exercise and exhilaration of her ride.

Christina nodded politely. She was trying to remember where she had last seen an old hand saw. Maybe in the toolshed? She wondered if it would be sharp enough to trim away the branches sticking up from the fallen tree.

"Helloooo, Christina. Are you still sleeping?" Anna joked.

"Hmm?" Christina murmured absently.

"What was the time on that, Joe?" Ian asked excitedly.

"I got him at a minute flat," the clocker called back.

"And I wasn't pushing him at all, Ian," Anna added. "He's got much more in him than that."

A small smile crossed the trainer's face "If he gets an even break in his first race, he'll be the horse to beat," Ian declared, his green eyes sparkling with excitement. "The horse has class."

"He sure does," Anna said admiringly. She leaned forward and stroked the colt's handsome neck. "You're lucky to own such a promising colt, Christina."

Christina tore her attention away from the tree and regarded the colt for a moment. He really was a majestic animal and he really did belong to her. Her parents had given her the colt for her twelfth birthday, but the truth was, she couldn't think of him as her horse. For one thing, she wasn't even allowed to ride him. For another, he wasn't a jumper. She knew Legacy was one of the most important horses on the farm, but as hard as she tried, she felt no special bond with him.

"C'mere, Legacy," she said halfheartedly, putting out a hand to pet him. But Legacy was still full of himself from his workout. He gave Christina a disdainful glance and pranced sideways.

"He never likes to stand still when he's on the track," Anna said apologetically. "Come see him in his stall after I cool him out," she called as she and Legacy waltzed away, the sweat beginning to steam on the horse's powerful hindquarters.

Christina gave a little wave, then folded her arms over the fence rail again and sighed. She watched the horse stride gracefully down the track toward the gap, and felt the tight ache in her throat that came every time she thought about her birthday, Christmas morning, the morning she'd gotten Legacy.

Christina had wanted her own horse more than anything. She was outgrowing her pony and her riding teacher said she was ready for more challenging jumps. For most of the past year she had artfully hounded her parents to get her a horse of her own. She had even done extra-credit school work to keep her grades up so they couldn't use that as an excuse not to buy her a horse. By Christmas, Christina was sure she had worn them down. She was going to get her dream horse—a horse she could jump, an Event horse.

On Christmas Eve, Christina went to bed joyous. She didn't think she could sleep, but her mind raced eagerly into a dream of a beautiful stone gray horse that stood on top of a flower-dotted hill, its silky mane ruffled by a warm breeze.

On Christmas morning, Christina's parents led her down to the stables. Christina could hardly contain herself. She was pretending to be puzzled for her parents' enjoyment, but she knew she was about to meet her very own horse. Would it be a bay or a gray? A mare or a gelding? It didn't matter, Christina decided. Soon she'd be riding her horse over a cross-country course. She grinned to herself, imagining how much trouble her parents must have gone through to ship the horse into the barn without her knowing it. Christina was elated! She actually skipped the last of the way down the hill to the barn. "You're the best parents in the whole world!" she exclaimed as they entered the stables.

"Happy Birthday, darling," her mother said. Then her father opened a stall door and lovingly presented her with the horse inside: Wonder's Legacy.

Christina's smile froze on her face for a moment, then nearly crumpled into a sob before she could stop it. She bit her lip ferociously to keep herself from losing control. Her parents were beaming at her and at each other. She saw her father slip his arm around her mother's shoulders and give her a hug.

"I know how much you've been wanting your

own horse," her mother said. "I wanted your first horse to be as special as mine was."

"I . . . I don't know what to say," Christina finally stammered. And she didn't. Legacy was Wonder's last foal. She knew her parents thought they had given her the best present in the world, but Christina didn't want a racehorse—she wanted an Event horse, one that she could begin riding right away.

She forced herself to go into the stall and pretend to make a fuss over Legacy. Numbly she felt her way around the colt's sturdy chest to his side where her face was hidden from her parents. There, at least, she could drop the phony smile. What a terrible mistake! She didn't want to seem ungrateful, but how could her parents have misunderstood? Hadn't they listened to her all those days when she talked about training her own horse to jump? Overwhelmed, she leaned her head against Legacy's sleek shoulder, pretending to pet him while she swiped furiously at the tears that kept forming in her eyes.

Somehow Christina got through the rest of the day without her parents catching on to how let down she felt. That evening, when all the opened gifts sat around the living room amid bits of tattered wrap and ribbon, and the bottom of the Christmas tree was bare and forlorn, she slipped away. The contented murmuring of her parents faded behind her as she crept up the attic stairs. At last she stood with relief in the little attic room, the place she always went when she was feeling down.

The room was in bluish shadows. Through two dormer windows on opposite sides, the cloudy sky was fading to the pale gray of early evening. An old floor lamp stood at the top of the stairs, but Christina didn't bother to turn it on. She had been coming to the attic since she was very small, and it was never scary to her, even in the dark. She moved surely through the boxes of stored junk and shrouded furniture, and found her way to the old, cracked leather chair in the corner. There, under the last glimmer of light from one of the dormers, she had pulled an old quilt over her knees, curled up in the ample arms of the old chair, and wept.

"What's the matter, Chris? You look as though you've got all the sorrows of the world upon your shoulders."

Christina's memory of her twelfth birthday faded as Ian spoke, but tears still glazed her eyes.

Ian continued to peer at her. "What's the matter?" he asked again, full of concern.

Christina quickly swiped at her eyes and managed a smile. "Oh, it's nothing," she assured him. "Allergies," she added, sniffing loudly. For good measure she sneezed.

Ian looked at her suspiciously. "Allergies, huh?" he said.

Christina glanced at her watch. "Gotta go," she

said, trying to sound cheerful. "I have a lesson at Mona's at ten."

She turned and fled to the stables, still wiping at her tears as she ran.

2

CHRISTINA SLOWED TO A BOUNCY, PURPOSEFUL WALK when she was out of Ian's sight and took a few deep breaths to calm herself, then headed toward the stables. All the buildings at Whitebrook were painted a soft warm red, trimmed with clean white. There were several outbuildings, and three large, long barns were arranged in a horseshoe shape. Christina's pony was stabled in the main barn in the center, but first she cut through the stallion barn, hoping to find Ian's son, Kevin. He could always cheer her up.

In the first stall on the right was Blues King, her father's big black Thoroughbred stallion. The stately horse had sired many winning racers in his sixteen years. Though he had sometimes been difficult to handle in his younger days, he had settled down in his teenage years to become as gentle and unflappable as an old school horse.

Christina opened the top half of the stall door. The horse stood gazing out the window that overlooked one of the paddocks where some of his offspring were playing. "Hey, Blue," Christina called softly. The wise old horse recognized the familiar voice and stepped toward her. Christina remembered visiting Blue when she was just a toddler, her father lifting her high so that she could reach his neck. He was big for a Thoroughbred—seventeen hands—and his conformation revealed the awesome power he had once displayed on the racetrack, but his large dark eyes were soft and kind. He arched his splendid neck and whuffed at Christina's outstretched hand. Christina smiled, moving to reach his massive jaw where he liked to be rubbed. As she did, she noticed that his black face was growing grayer around his eyes and his soft muzzle.

"Gotta go, Blue," she told the gentle stallion. "But I'll bring you a treat later. I promise." She stroked his neck once more and closed the door.

She strode down the aisle, ignoring the reactions of some of the more aggressive stallions who stomped and pawed angrily as she passed. The worst was a stallion her father had bought in a claiming race a few years back. He was a big dark gray known as The Terminator. When Christina passed his stall she couldn't resist slowing down to gaze at the fierce stallion. She knew better than to tease him, although when she was younger she and Kevin McLean used to dare each other to see who would get closest to Terminator's stall.

The Terminator stood his ground, alert but still, his dark eyes on Christina. Mesmerized by his intense gaze, Christina took a step toward his stall. He continued to stare at her. Feeling bold, Christina took another step toward him, and then another, feeling a delicious thrill of fear as she inched closer.

"Looking for trouble?" said a boy's voice.

Christina turned and saw Kevin coming toward her. Kevin McLean never walked—he bounded. His tousled auburn hair and deep green eyes were exactly like his father's. He was just five months younger than Christina. The two had grown up together at Whitebrook and were practically like brother and sister. With her parents busy with the farm and her mother's career as a jockey, Christina had spent so much time at the McLeans' cottage that she considered it a second home. And Beth McLean, Kevin's mother, had spent almost as much time caring for Christina as her own parents had.

"Hi, Kev," Christina said, smiling.

"You're not terrorizing The Terminator, are you?" Kevin asked her.

"Me?" Christina said innocently. "Of course not."

"Well, you better get out of here before Mr. Ballard catches you. I saw him heading this way," Kevin warned her. George Ballard was the manager of the stallion barn. Christina knew a person had to be tough to handle stallions, but Mr. Ballard was beyond tough. When she was little, just the sight of his stern face used to make her cry. If Mr. Ballard caught her and Kevin messing with The Terminator, he'd probably chase them off the property with a longe whip!

Just then they heard footsteps crunching in the gravel outside the barn door.

"Let's go," Christina hissed, and she and Kevin hurried toward the door at the opposite end of the barn, walking as fast as they could without running.

"What are you kids doing in there?" Mr. Ballard's gruff voice carried all the way down the aisle.

"Run," Christina whispered to Kevin, and the two of them tumbled out the barn door and bolted for safety.

"There!" Kevin charged toward a dense tangle of forsythia bushes covered with yellow blooms.

Christina followed him, and she and Kevin dove for cover behind the bushes just seconds before Mr. Ballard appeared in the barn door.

"Duck," Kevin hissed, pulling Christina down behind the thick branches at the bottom of the bushes. Christina began to giggle uncontrollably. Kevin clapped a hand over her mouth and she continued to shake with silent laughter until Mr. Ballard gave up and went back in the barn, muttering to himself.

When he was out of sight, Kevin took his hand off

Christina's mouth. "I think you owe me one," he commented.

"Okay." Christina nodded soberly. Then without warning she set her shoulder against Kevin's chest and pushed hard. He fell over backward and Christina tackled him, trying to pin him down.

Kevin was big for his age and outweighed Christina by several pounds, but this time his weight went against him. The ground sloped slightly and Christina had pinned him with his head downhill. Kevin tried to twist out from under her, but she was leaning on his shoulders with all her might. With his legs higher than his head, Kevin was trapped.

A second later Christina had both his shoulders pinned to the grass. "I pinned you! I pinned you!" she crowed triumphantly. She and Kevin had been wrestling each other since they were in kindergarten. For a long time Christina had been taller and could beat him every time, but Kevin had finally caught up with her. Now it took careful strategy for Christina to get the upper hand.

"Okay, you got me that time," Kevin agreed good-naturedly. "Now would you mind letting me up?"

"Oh, I don't know," Christina teased him. "I'm kind of enjoying this." She peered at Kevin's familiar face, with its sprinkle of freckles across his nose. "Your face is turning red," she added.

"Come on, Chris. The grass is wet," Kevin complained.

"Whiner," Christina called him, but she relented. Laughing and panting, the two got to their feet, and began brushing off the dirt and grass from their jeans.

"Want to go for a ride?" Kevin asked as they began walking toward the training barn.

"I have a lesson at Mona's," Christina told him. "How about this afternoon?"

"Okay," Kevin said. "Around three?"

"Sure," Christina agreed.

"See you later, then," Kevin said. He bounded off in the direction of the McLeans' cottage.

Christina watched him go, then checked her watch. If she hurried, she would still have time to pay a quick visit to Faith and Shining Moment. She headed for the training barn.

Leap of Faith was a chestnut filly her father had bought at an auction two summers ago. Faith had been a skinny, bedraggled youngster, owned by a disreputable New Jersey farm. The owner, an amateur in the horse business, had raced the filly unsuccessfully as a two-year-old and then put her up for auction. Christina remembered how Ian McLean and some of the barn staff had teased her father when he brought the scrawny filly home, but he had seen potential in the filly's flawless conformation. When Ian and Ashleigh asked why he'd bought such a scraggly youngster, Mike had just shrugged and said that sometimes in the horse business you had to make a leap of faith, which was how Faith got her name. He said that very often a younger, less-developed two-year-old might grow into a talented racer as a three-year-old, and that's just what had happened with Faith.

Christina was captivated by her father's explanation. Her mother was practical when it came to horses. Most professional horse people were. But her father was more of a dreamer and a risk taker, and Christina took after him. The idea of making a leap of faith sounded mysterious to her and somehow magical, as if, by caring enough to believe in something, she might help make it happen. Maybe one day she would see an unlikely looking horse that nobody wanted and it would turn out to be just the horse for her.

Christina reached over the stall guard to stroke the filly. She had a dainty white star on her forehead that lit up her gorgeous face. "Hi, Faith," Christina said in a soft voice that made the filly's perfect ears prick forward with interest. "Hi, pretty girl. Had your workout yet?" Christina asked, sliding her hand down the mare's silky neck.

Christina loved the feel of the young horses' coats under her hand. She stroked Faith's satin chest, pausing for a moment to feel the strong, steady pounding of the filly's heart. Thoroughbreds were all sinew and bone and muscle, built to battle the track and slice through the wind, and inside them was a coiled energy that was always ready to burst out. But their skins were thin and supple, and their coats were pure silk, especially the colts and fillies. Faith's shiny, well-groomed shoulder was as impossibly soft as an old silky robe of her mother's that Christina loved to wear.

When she'd finished visiting Faith, Christina moved to the next stall where Shining Moment stood. The strawberry roan colt had the look of his dam, Shining, another former Whitebrook champion who happened to be Wonder's half sister. Shining, now a brood mare at Whitebrook, belonged to the McLeans' daughter and Kevin's older sister, Samantha.

Christina remembered Samantha well, though she hadn't seen her since Samantha had moved to Ireland six years ago. Samantha and Ashleigh were close friends and still called each other often. Lately Samantha had been suggesting that the Reeses visit her in Ireland. Christina was dying to go. She knew that Ireland was one of the best places to ride cross-country, and outstanding Event horses were bred there. She could just imagine cantering across a strip of beach in Ireland, her horse's hooves splashing in the shallow, sparkling surf.

Then Shining Moment stomped, startling Christina out of her daydream. "You scared me," Christina scolded the mischievous three-year-old. She reached over the stall guard to scratch his neck affectionately. Christina liked the horse's unusual red-and-white coloring, which turned him a rosy gold when the sun hit him just right. His four perfectly white stockings looked as though he'd dipped each leg in a bucket of paint. She let him nibble at her hair until he nipped playfully at her and she had to jerk out of the way. "Hey!" Christina chided him. "None of that, now."

Christina headed out of the training barn and followed the gravel path to the third barn, where the mares and foals were stabled. Inside, grooms and handlers were busy with the endless chores involved with running a stable. Christina said polite hellos, paused to give Shining a quick pat, then headed down the aisle to the last stall on the left, which housed her mother's old mare, Wonder.

"Hi, Wonder," Christina said fondly. She slipped under the stall guard and went to stand beside the graceful chestnut mare who nickered a welcome. Wonder was twenty-four years old now, and under her blanket her back dipped down between her withers and her croup, the result of carrying foals for many years. But except for how her back had dropped, Wonder showed no other signs of her age. Her sleek legs were as clean as ever, and her brown eyes were clear and sparkling with life. She nickered again as Christina hugged her slender neck, then nuzzled the girl affectionately.

Of all the Thoroughbreds at Whitebrook, Wonder was the only one her mother had ever let her ride. Early in her life Christina had sensed a connection between her mother and Wonder, a connection that somehow went beyond the love and devotion ordinarily shared by a horse and its owner. Coming into Wonder's stall always felt to Christina like coming home. She knew every crack in the white-painted boards, and the warm clean smell of the old horse was as familiar to her as buttered toast. Her mother had traveled often when Christina was young, and whenever Christina missed her, she would wander over to Wonder's stall for comfort. More than once, her father had come looking for her and found her asleep on the clean straw piled in the corner of the stall, the horse standing guard over her as if she were one of her foals.

Christina laid her cheek against Wonder's neck for a moment. "I wish you could tell Mom how I feel," she whispered.

Wonder snorted softly, as if encouraging Christina to go on.

"Legacy's a wonderful colt," Christina told the old mare. "But you know Mom. She's so overprotective. She won't even let me ride him."

Wonder shook her head gently as if she simply couldn't believe it.

Christina stroked Wonder's neck and whispered to the horse. "You understand, don't you, girl? It's not that I don't appreciate Legacy. It's just that I want an Event horse, a big gray mare with dark dapples and a silvery mane." She combed her fingers through

Wonder's reddish mane. "I'll canter her up to some kind of huge jump—maybe a big log, or a brush pile," she went on. "And we'll sail over it. It'll be like flying," Christina said dreamily.

Wonder nodded her head.

Christina put her arms around the old mare's neck. "I wish my mom and dad understood as well as you do."

3

IN THE STALL ACROSS FROM WONDER'S WAS CHRISTINA'S pony, a pretty brown-and-white paint. His official show name was Tribulation, but he was known around the barn as "Trouble," and to Christina as "Tribbles," or simply "Trib." Christina grabbed a hoof pick and went into the pony's stall.

As she picked out his feet, Christina thought about all the work she'd put into Trib since she got him three years ago. Once she had outgrown her first pony, her riding teacher, Mona Gardener, had been on the lookout for another pony for her, one that moved well and showed promise as a jumper. One day she had spotted Tribbles grazing in a pasture with a herd of cows on a neighboring farm. Mona had asked about the pony and was told that he had proved to be too much for the child he'd been bought for and that nobody would buy him.

Mona told the Reeses about the pony and they all drove to the farm to see him. Christina would never forget seeing Trib for the first time. He was covered with mud and was standing in a herd of cows as if he thought he was one. Christina remembered how the pony had looked her in the eye and trotted around her in a perfect circle, showing off his moves. Christina had fallen in love with him then and there.

The owner was honest. "That pony's a bad bucker," he warned them. But when Christina rode the pony that day, he was a perfect angel. They ended up taking him home.

But soon it was obvious that Tribbles had been on his best behavior that day. He quickly earned his name, proving himself to be as terrible as he was beautiful. Her first horse show with Trib was a disaster. To Christina's dismay, the pony bolted, bucked, refused, rushed, and generally spent all his energy trying to unseat her.

"Christina, I think we made a mistake. That pony needs so much work," Mona said a few months later at another show. Christina had just been excused from the ring for the third time. "He's gorgeous when he's good, but mostly he's just useless. Let's find you something with better manners. Aren't you tired of getting asked to leave the showring for being out of control?"

"Nope," Christina said adamantly. "And I wasn't out of control. I was just letting him get his bucks out."

Mona rolled her eyes and threw up her hands in mock defeat.

Christina refused to give up on Trib. She rode the pony with a gritty determination that was an equal match for his antics. No matter how high he bucked, or how fast he bolted, Christina stuck to him like glue. Fixed in her mind was the image of herself riding Trib that day in the cow pasture, when he'd been absolutely perfect. And finally, under Christina's patient guidance, the pony began to settle down.

As she picked up his last foot and began scooping the dirt out of it, Christina remembered how proud she'd felt when she and Trib finally had their first flawless round in a pony hunter class in a big A-rated show. And then how down she'd felt when they didn't even win a ribbon. Mona had explained that paint horses often didn't win in hunter classes, simply because their coloring wasn't traditional.

She had done better in the pony jumpers, where they were judged on speed and penalized for "faults"—knocking down or refusing a fence. Christina loved the speed and quick turns, but the jumps weren't very big—only two-six or two-nine. Most ponies couldn't jump much higher than that. Christina knew she was ready for more. She set down Trib's foot and rapped the hoof pick against the stall wall to clean it. She had come a long way with Trib and she still loved him, but looking at his straight but short legs, she knew she had outgrown him. On a horse she could easily clear the big three- or four-foot cross-country jumps.

Christina ran a currycomb over her pony's sleek coat, then went over him again with a brush, giving an expert flip of her wrist at the end of each stroke to lift the dirt and hair loosened by the comb. Every curve and muscle of his sturdy body was as familiar to her as her own hands. Next she smoothed his coat with a soft dandy brush. When she had given him a final wipe with a rub rag, she stood back, eyeing her grooming job. Not bad.

Christina spread the fluffy, clean pad on Trib's back and laid her saddle on top of it, fastening the girth loosely. The bridle was hanging over her shoulder. She slipped the reins over the pony's head, then gently stuck her thumb and finger into the corners of his mouth until he opened up and accepted the bit. She pulled the crownpiece over his ears, fastened the noseband, and was ready to go. She started to lead him out of the stall, but then paused for a moment. The pony was gazing soulfully at her with his big brown eyes, earnest creases of kindness above them. It was the same look that had captivated her the very first time she had seen him. Instantly Christina's heart melted. She stroked his nose and gave him a big kiss right between the eyes.

There was a mounting block carved from a chunk of stone just outside the barn, but Christina didn't bother to use it. She stuck her left foot into the stirrup and swung into the saddle easily. Then she turned Trib toward the driveway that led down to the main road.

Usually she would have taken the longer route to Mona's, through the back pasture and across two neighboring farms. It was a much prettier ride, but she'd be late if she went that way today. It was quicker to go the mile and a half to Mona's straight along the main road. At the bottom of the driveway, she turned onto the wide shoulder of the quiet road and picked up a posting trot.

Christina was on guard for a playful buck or spook from Trib. Sometimes he still cut up a little when she first got on him, but all he did was shake his head a few times, as if shrugging off the urge to be impish. Then he settled right down to business, without any of his usual morning antics.

Trib's steady trot quickly ate up the distance. In no time at all Christina spotted the sign at the bottom of the driveway that led to Mona's stables. "Gardener Farm," the sign read, with the outline of a jumping horse painted underneath. Christina asked her pony to walk. She carefully looked both right and left, and when she was sure no cars were coming, she crossed the road and started up the driveway to Mona's place.

When she reached the end of the drive, she could see that Mona was already down in the big arena, setting up a jump course. Christina walked over to the arena and through the open gate. "Hi, Mona," she called cheerfully to her trainer.

"Good morning, Christina," Mona said. Mona Gardener was five and a half feet tall, muscular and wiry, with short brown hair and clear gray eyes. Though it was early in the spring, she already had a light, healthy tan from being outside so much.

Christina felt her spirits lift instantly as she entered the familiar arena. She was happiest when she was having a riding lesson. She could not think of any place she'd rather be. Mona had been teaching Christina since she was four years old and Christina practically worshipped her. Mona was her mother's best friend, but even if she hadn't been, it wouldn't have made a difference. Christina thought Mona was the best dressage and jumper rider she had ever seen. She hoped one day to be as strong and elegant a rider as Mona.

"Are you warmed up?" Mona asked as she moved a jump cup down several notches and secured it with the pin.

"We trotted most of the way," Christina said. "Let me just canter him a little, though." She gathered up her reins. "He was too good on the way over—I think he might still have a buck in him."

Mona laughed. "You're finally learning!" she said as she set the blue-and-white striped rail into the jump cup. "Never trust a pony."

Trib cantered once around the whole ring perfectly. Then, just as Christina was beginning a second circuit, a squirrel scurried up one of the fence rails and perched there, about to nibble on an acorn. Suddenly another squirrel ran up after him, and the first squirrel chattered angrily and dashed down the fence rail right into Trib and Christina's path. Trib dropped his head toward the dirt and plunged sideways, twisting and bucking hard with every stride.

Trib's first buck had tipped Christina forward, jerking a rein out of her hand, and she'd lost one stirrup. She wasn't worried about the stirrup, but she was off balance, tipping dangerously forward and gripping with her knees. She groped uselessly for the other rein. Without it she had no control over the pony's erratic sideways course. She caught a glimpse of Mona's jeans and paddock boots as Trib lurched across the middle of the ring.

"Sit up, Chris! Get your eyes up!" Mona yelled.

Christina snapped her chin up. As soon as her eyes were up, she found she could sit back in the saddle, and her frown of concentration turned into a look of amused confidence.

"Ha!" she said triumphantly. "Humans one, ponies zero!" She picked up the rein she had dropped and gave it a firm tug as she closed her lower legs around the pony's sides. Two more tugs brought his head up. Quickly she shortened the reins and straightened him. Then she felt his hindquarters come down under him, and his bucking subsided. Christina relaxed and slipped her foot into the stirrup she had lost. Then she cantered smoothly on as if nothing had happened.

"Are you okay?" Mona called.

"Just fine," Christina said cheerfully.

"Good job," Mona told her, and went on setting up fences.

When she had made three more laps around the arena in the other direction, Christina made a transition to a walk and brought Trib over to Mona, who was standing in the middle of the ring. The pony was breathing a little hard from his work, but the look in his eye was calm. He snorted a few times, then stood still, looking glad to have a rest.

Christina looked at Mona for approval and saw it in her face. "I told you he felt like he might have a buck in him," she said, and giggled.

"No kidding," Mona said. "That was an amazing recovery. That pony was bucking and twisting like a rodeo horse. I think he would have gotten me off. Sometimes I don't know how you do it, Christina."

Christina considered for a moment. "Sometimes I don't know, either," she admitted. She had fallen off Trib a few times, but not as often as people expected when they saw how the pony could act up. Christina patted Trib's neck. "Rotten pony," she said fondly.

"Okay, let's get to work," Mona said. "Pick up a trot and start warming up over that crossrail."

Christina began jumping the X. After a couple of times over it, Mona stopped her. "Aren't your stirrups a little short?" she asked, frowning as she scrutinized Christina's leg position.

Christina pushed her heels down so her legs would look a little longer. "I kind of have to keep them short," she said sheepishly. "Last week when I was jumping I kept bumping my heels on the rails."

Mona gazed at Christina's long legs scrunched up with the short stirrups to fit around the pony's sides. "You've really outgrown him," Mona said with a sigh.

As usual, once Trib had gotten his bucks out, he was perfect. Christina spent a blissful forty-five minutes jumping her pony. Mona gave her a challenging course, with a rollback turn where she had to land from one fence, then almost sit Trib down on his haunches and spin him around to jump the next fence. She jumped the course three times, and the last time was as close to perfect as she could have wanted.

"Good boy," Christina said, hugging her pony's neck. She let the reins all the way out to the buckle and took her feet out of the stirrups. With her long legs dangling, she could almost hook her toes together under his belly. She could just imagine how big she must look on him. Tribbles walked along placidly, looking completely incapable of the wild streak he had displayed less than an hour before.

"That was excellent, Christina," Mona said approvingly.

"I just wish we could jump higher," Christina said. Wistfully she eyed the section of cross-country jump course that was visible on the hill on the north side of the arena. There was a brush jump that must have been four feet wide and three feet high. Christina had to imagine how it must feel to jump over big fences like that.

"I know," Mona said. "You're definitely ready to move up in height. I've been thinking, Christina. You've pretty much done all you can do with Trib. I know you want to get into Eventing, but that pony's just too little to take around a big cross-country course. You need a horse."

"No kidding," Christina said. "But we know that's not likely to happen right away. Unless for some reason Wonder's Legacy turns out to be a dud."

Mona gave Christina a sympathetic look. "Chris, I know how you feel about that whole incident, but remember, your mom was really trying to please you. Believe me, it just never occurred to her that her own daughter wouldn't be interested in owning a racehorse."

"Well, she knows I don't want to be a jockey," Christina went on. "I mean, I'm not exactly built like one. I'm already almost too tall and heavy."

31

"That doesn't mean you can't enjoy training or exercising your Thoroughbred. Believe me, Christina, your mother and father put a lot of thought into that gift. Your mother loves you and wants only the best for you."

"Sometimes that's hard to believe," Christina said softly, staring at the ground.

"I'm sure it feels that way," Mona said. She looked Christina straight in the eye. "Your mom works very hard, and even though she's not always around, it doesn't mean she doesn't love you."

Christina sighed. "I know. It's just so hard to get her attention. She gets so into her work that sometimes I feel like I could jump up and down on the dinner table and she still wouldn't notice me."

"She's very dedicated, Christina. And dedication is something she understands and admires. If you want her to understand and believe in your love for jumping and dressage, you've got to demonstrate it to her. Show her you're serious and professional and she'll drop everything to help you pursue your dream," Mona said. "She'll be your biggest fan—I guarantee it."

"Even if my dream isn't the same as hers might be?" Christina asked.

"Yes, Christina. Your mom wants you to be happy." Mona paused and tucked a strand of Christina's hair behind her ear. "So here's what I'm thinking. You're doing well with your flatwork. Last week when we practiced that dressage test you couldn't have done it any better. I think you're definitely ready to tackle a training-level dressage test at a show. And we know you're ready with the jumping. There's an Event coming up in a few weeks, over at Foxwood Acres. I think you should go. The only way your mom's going to respect your interest in Eventing is if we get you competing and get her to watch you."

"Really?" Christina asked. She felt a flutter of excitement at the thought of trying an Event for the very first time. "But I thought you said I couldn't really do an Event with Trib because the jumps would be too big for him."

Mona shook her head. "I don't mean with Trib."

"Then who?" Christina asked.

"What would you say to riding Foster?" Mona said, flashing Christina a big smile.

"Oh, Mona, do you mean it?" Foster was Mona's Irish Thoroughbred, a big black gelding who could jump the moon. Mona often competed with him in three-day events, and the two of them had twice qualified to be shortlisted for the United States Olympic Team. Christina had admired the big gelding for years, but she'd never imagined that Mona would let her ride him, never mind compete with him in an Event.

Mona nodded. "Of course I mean it. Next week you can start working with him. If you get along, you can ride him in the Event. Does that sound okay to you?" Mona asked.

"Okay?" Christina said in disbelief. "It's more than okay—it's incredible! It's unbelievable! Oh, thank you, Mona!" Christina jumped off of Trib and threw her arms around Mona's neck. "Thank you, thank you, thank you!"

"Well, don't thank me yet. You might not like him at all," Mona cautioned her.

Christina gave Mona a skeptical look. "I'm going to love him. I know it!"

4

"KATIE!" CHRISTINA CALLED TO HER BEST FRIEND AS SHE scurried into the barn.

Katie Garrity, a pretty, willowy girl with ash-blond hair, was grooming a horse on crossties in the aisle. She looked up from her work and peered around the horse's head when she heard her name. "Hi, Chris," she called. Christina and Katie had known each other since the second grade. "What's up?" Katie asked curiously, reading the excitement in Christina's face.

Christina was beaming as she led Trib carefully under another horse's crosstie and then hurried toward her friend. "Mona's going to let me ride Foster!" Christina announced.

"Really?" Katie said. "That's great! When?"

"Next week. I get to try him out in a lesson, and if we get along, I'm going to take him in an Event at

Foxwood Acres. I'm finally going to get to jump some big jumps!" Christina crowed. "Isn't that wonderful?"

"That's great news," Katie said enthusiastically. "That means we can train together, because Seabreeze and I are going in the Event, too. Aren't we, girl?" Katie began going over the shiny bay mare with a soft dandy brush.

"I'm so excited," Christina said. "I don't see how I can wait until next week to ride him."

"Why don't you get on him right now?"

Christina spun around and saw Mona standing with her hands on her hips.

"Could I?" Christina could hardly believe it.

"Sure. Either you can ride him or you can't. We might as well find out," Mona said. "I asked Matt to tack him for you. It'll just be a few minutes. Bring him on down to the ring as soon as you're ready. Okay?"

"Okay," Christina said. "But what should I do with Trib?"

"You can stick him in that empty stall down at the end for now," Mona told her. "Untack him and throw him a flake of hay. Matt will fill the water bucket."

Christina untacked her pony and put him in the empty stall. Then she tossed him a flake of hay and went to get Foster. Matt, the head groom, stood waiting patiently for Christina, holding the big black gelding. "So, you're going to ride the big boy today, huh?" Matt asked Christina.

Christina nodded, smiling happily. "I guess so," she said.

Foster tossed his head as if he thought it was a fine idea, and Christina laughed. She patted his shining, muscular shoulder. "Ready, Foster?" she asked.

Matt led Foster out of the barn, then handed the reins to Christina. "Here you go," Matt said.

"Thank you," Christina said politely.

Christina looked up at Foster. The horse towered above her; he had to be close to seventeen hands high. Christina had to stand on tiptoe to put the reins over his head. Then she tried getting her left foot into the stirrup to mount up, but she couldn't get her foot that high. She looked around for a mounting block, then remembered that Mona kept one down in the ring. She wished she'd asked Matt for a leg up. Now she'd have to lead Foster down to the ring and mount up there.

"Want a leg up?" It was Dylan Becker, a boy from school who also rode at Gardener Farm. Christina knew him. He was one of the most popular boys in the seventh grade at Henry Clay Middle School. He had close-cropped curly brown hair and brown eyes, and he was wearing a pair of sand-colored chaps with blue piping and fringes. Christina couldn't help admiring them. She was pretty sure they were custom-made. Then it occurred to her that it wasn't just the chaps she liked, but the way Dylan looked in them. She looked down so he wouldn't see her blush.

She had seen Dylan plenty of times at Mona's. He had never paid any attention to her before. Suddenly Christina was nervous. Dylan was still standing there, waiting for her to answer him.

"Sure. That would be great," Christina said. "He's so tall." She gathered the reins in her left hand and faced the saddle, her left knee bent. She felt Dylan take her leg in his hands.

"You count," Dylan said.

"One, two, three," Christina counted, and sprung toward the saddle.

Dylan boosted her way too hard and she nearly went over the other side of the horse headfirst. Suddenly she was high over Foster's back, her weight on her hands and her left knee, which Dylan still held. She couldn't sit down because he was still holding her leg up. Then she realized that Dylan was grinning as if he thought it was pretty funny. Had he tried to throw her over the off side on purpose? It was an old trick. She and Kevin had done it to each other many times.

"Hey, let me down," Christina said indignantly. Dylan lowered her leg until she was sitting in the saddle. "Thanks," Christina said sarcastically.

"Sorry. I didn't mean to throw you so high," Dylan said. "You're light as a feather."

Christina felt the blood rush to her face again. Was he kidding? She kept her eyes on the stirrup leather she was adjusting and said nothing.

"How come you're riding Foster? Aren't you the girl with that crazy paint pony?" Dylan asked her.

She decided to answer the first question and ignore the second. "Mona said I could," Christina told him, adjusting the other stirrup. She was still flustered from her less-than-graceful experience with the leg up. Her ears felt as if they were on fire. "I might take him in an Event at Foxwood Acres."

"I didn't know you competed in Eventing," Dylan said.

Christina finished adjusting the stirrups and managed to look him in the eye. "Well, I haven't done an actual Event yet, but I've been working on the training-level dressage tests. I'm going to try jumping Foster over some of the cross-country fences, and if we do well, I'll take him to Foxwood."

"Cool," Dylan said. "I might be going to that Event," he added.

"Oh," Christina said. "Have you competed in lots of Events?"

"Nope," Dylan said. "It'll be my first Event, too. Looks like we're in it together," he said with a friendly smile.

Christina couldn't help smiling back. She glanced down at the ring and saw that Katie was already jumping Seabreeze. "I better get going," she said. "Mona's waiting for us."

"See you later," Dylan said, and sauntered into the barn without a backward glance.

Christina rode Foster down to the arena, pausing at the in-gate while Katie and Seabreeze cantered past. Then she began walking the big black gelding around the ring while she waited for Mona to tell her what to do. Christina was so used to riding ponies that at first sitting on the big Thoroughbred was like being on another planet. For one thing, Foster had a lively, active walk that felt worlds different from Trib's pony-legged walk. For another, her view of the arena was entirely different. It felt strange to be riding with her head so far above the fence rail. It reminded her of riding in the cab of her parents' big truck, compared with when she rode in her dad's little sports car. But in a few minutes Christina decided that she preferred the view from up high.

"Katie, your last line was gorgeous, but I want to see you do the whole course one more time," Mona was saying. "This time do the bending line in seven strides instead of six, and then when you're coming to the single fence, don't try to do so much. Long approaches are easier if you just let the fence come to you," Mona instructed.

Christina watched while Katie organized herself and then picked up a canter and began the course again. The fences were set at three feet—six inches higher than the course Christina had been jumping. Christina watched with admiration as Seabreeze's graceful strides seemed to float her around the ring, barely touching the ground. The beautiful seven-year-old Thoroughbred was "off the track," which meant that she had been a racehorse before the Garritys bought her for Katie. Christina wondered briefly if Legacy would be able to jump like that.

When Katie had finished the course, Mona praised her and told her to walk Seabreeze out. "Okay, Christina," she said. "Go ahead and pick up a trot."

Christina pressed her calves against Foster's sides and he trotted on. Christina began to post. But she was unprepared for how differently Foster moved compared to her pony. Trib was a "daisy cutter," who swung his legs in smooth, flat, comfortable strides at the trot, hardly bending his knees. Foster's powerful hindquarters and long legs thrust his back in a high arc with each springy stride of his trot. Christina felt as though she was being thrown all over the place. She struggled to keep her legs steady and tried to control her posting, but she just couldn't seem to get comfortable. Then, as she trotted around the turn by the in-gate, she noticed Dylan Becker sitting on the fence watching her.

"You look good on him," Dylan said to her, smiling as she bounced past him.

Christina felt her face go all hot and tingly with embarrassment. Surely he was joking. She knew she must look terrible. She clenched her teeth and doubled her efforts to look smooth on Foster's terrible bouncy trot, and somehow, by her second time around the ring, she had begun to feel a little more capable.

"Feel like you're getting used to him now?" Mona asked her as she trotted by.

Christina nodded. By the third time around the ring she still thought he was bouncy, but she felt she was posting smoothly.

"All right then. See how you like his canter," Mona told her.

Christina squeezed her fingers on the reins, signaling Foster to walk. He was "heavy" in her hands compared to Trib. Christina felt as if she had to use a lot more strength in her arms and back to get the transition, but when she did, Foster obeyed her right away. It was a relief to sit still for a moment. Christina felt a flutter of nervousness somewhere between her stomach and her heart. What would Foster's canter be like? Would it be as bouncy as his trot? Would the big horse be difficult to control? She glanced toward the end of the ring and saw that Dylan was still watching her.

"Go ahead, Chris," Mona said. "Canter on."

Christina took a deep breath and let it out slowly, trying to keep her arms and her back relaxed so that the horse wouldn't pick up on her anxiety. Then she shortened her reins and gave Foster a bump with her outside leg, dreading what would happen next.

To her amazement, the horse cantered flawlessly right out of the walk, and his canter was as smooth as syrup and so different from what she was used to. Trib's legs drummed the ground in his short pony strides when he cantered, so that she felt every footfall, but on Foster, she was far above the ground and the three-beat thrust of his legs was muted in rhythm and power. Sitting on Foster's canter was as easy as riding the swells in the ocean. She came around the turn where Dylan stood and this time she saw unmistakable admiration in his face as she swept by. When her back was to him, a big smile broke over her face, and she knew she could ride this horse, bouncy trot and all. She was going to be just fine.

The ride on Foster was over much too soon for Christina. After that canter she could have stayed on him forever. For the rest of the day, Christina couldn't stop thinking about how much fun it had been. She told Kevin all about it later that afternoon as they rode along the fence line in one of the pastures at Whitebrook.

"And she let me try jumping him, too," Christina said enthusiastically.

"How high did you jump?" Kevin wanted to know.

"Not very high," Christina admitted. "Just a crossrail and then a little vertical. But I'm going to jump higher," she assured him. She'd wanted to jump the course that Katie was jumping, or at least a couple of fences, but Mona said she had to get used to jumping Foster over smaller fences first.

"That's great," Kevin said.

They rode along in silence for a while, enjoying the sunshine and the clean smell of the early spring air. Tribbles stepped along contentedly beside Kevin's sorrel gelding, Jasper. Jasper was an Anglo-Arab: a Thoroughbred crossed with an Arabian. His light chestnut coat shone over his rippling muscles, and his creamy mane streamed from his arched neck. Christina watched the two horses' heads bobbing in time with their walk. Then she began to imagine what it might be like to be riding along like this with Dylan. "Do you know Dylan Becker?" she asked Kevin.

"Sure," Kevin said. "He's on the basketball team and I play baseball with him in the summer. He's pretty good," Kevin added. "Why?"

"No reason," Christina said. Kevin was looking curiously at her, making her wish she hadn't said anything. Before them, twenty yards away, was a wooded section of the pasture. "Hey, you want to do the steeplechase course?" Christina said, glad for a chance to change the subject.

"Okay," Kevin agreed. "The winner has to buy sodas."

"Deal," Christina said.

"But I warn you," Kevin said mischievously, "I have a need for speed."

"No fear," Christina said coolly as she gathered up Trib's reins. The pony's ears pricked forward as he

44

anticipated what was about to happen. "Ready?" Christina asked Kevin.

"Just say when," Kevin said, poised to gallop.

"Go!" Christina yelled.

Christina and Trib took off across the grass toward the trees, with Kevin and his horse right beside them. The steeplechase course was really a trail through the trees across which Christina and Kevin had placed obstacles. They had been racing each other over the course since they were old enough to ride by themselves. They tore across the last stretch of pasture, manes and tails flying.

The steeplechase course wasn't wide enough for two horses to ride abreast. Once they were actually on the trail, they would have to go single file, so usually whoever was in front when they hit the woods would be the winner. Jasper and Trib were neck and neck as they galloped toward the trees. Christina bent low over Tribbles's neck, urging him on. But then Jasper began to pull ahead and Christina had to check Trib at the entrance to the path to keep from bumping Jasper's hindquarters as he dodged ahead of them into the trees.

"Shoot!" Christina grumbled.

"Gotcha!" she heard Kevin holler as Jasper thundered down the trail in front of her.

"Not for long!" she yelled as Trib pounded after them.

Jasper sailed over the first obstacle: the low,

smooth trunk of a tree that had fallen across the trail. Trib sprung over it right behind him. Several strides further on was a small pile of brush and branches. Both horse and pony bounded over it. The third jump was just a tree branch they had set across the path, its ends resting in the low branches of the bushes on either side of the path. It was little more than a stick about two and a half feet high, with nothing but air under it, but Jasper and Trib knew it was there and cleared it without missing a beat.

In the straight stretch after the branch jump, Christina and Trib began to gain on Kevin and Jasper. The gelding's flaxen tail was nearly in Trib's face as they headed for an upcoming turn. She moved up on his inside as they headed into a bend in the path, and Christina clucked at Trib and moved her hands forward, asking him for a burst of speed.

The pony seemed to understand what she wanted and he doubled his strides, surging past Jasper on the inside of the turn and ducking in front of the horse just as the path straightened out and narrowed again.

"Hey!" Kevin cried out indignantly. "You little sneak!"

Howling with laughter, Christina and her pony flew over the next jump: two fir trees with their tops pointing at each other across the trail. Jasper's nose was inches from Trib's tail as they came to the last jump: a pile of tree branches. After that the trail widened. Kevin tried moving up on her, but she heard him on her left side and moved Tribbles to the left, blocking his path.

"Shoot!" Kevin grumbled behind her as she cut him off.

Christina giggled uncontrollably. Three strides after they cleared the branch pile, Christina broke through the trees into the sunlight again. In front of her was the homestretch, a long lane of grass leading to the top of a hill.

"Come on, Tribbles," she said to her pony. She glanced over her shoulder and saw Kevin right behind her, a determined grin on his face. "Eat my dust, McLean," she called back to him.

She dug her legs into Trib's sides and thundered up the stretch, sure she had Kevin beat. But when she glanced over her shoulder, she saw that Jasper was right beside her and moving up, his longer legs slowly but surely outstriding Trib.

Kevin was laughing as they pulled past. "See ya later when your legs are straighter," he said over his shoulder.

"Get up!" Christina ordered Trib, and gave him a smack on the shoulder with her bat. The pony shook his head in annoyance, but then seemed to dig in and find more speed. Trib's mane stung Christina's face as she leaned into his gallop, trying to get over the crest of the hill before Kevin.

Christina's eyes were tearing as she squinted into the sun and wind. Suddenly she saw a dark shape looming before her as she came over the rise. For a moment she couldn't think what it might be; then she remembered the fallen tree she had seen from the training oval that morning. The tree was directly in their path. Kevin was on her left. In that position he could easily move over and go the shorter distance around the broken stump of the tree. Christina realized she would either have to drop back and follow him, or go all the way around the top of the tree to her right. Either way, she would lose. Kevin glanced over at her, and she could see he was thinking the same thing. Then she had an idea.

"You're not beating me," Christina muttered. She shortened her reins a little and headed right for the trunk of the tree. Several leafy branches stuck up from the trunk, but there was one narrow section that was clear. It was easily three feet high, but somehow it just looked jumpable. She bore down on the tree, confident that Trib would be able to clear it.

Then they reached the tree. Kevin went to the left, around the stump, and Christina fixed her eyes on the trunk. Trib cantered all the way to the base of it without missing a beat. Christina rested her hands on the crest of his neck, prepared to feel him spring into the air and over the tree. She was already grinning, thinking how surprised Kevin would be when he came around the stump and saw that she had jumped the tree and pulled ahead of him.

The next thing she knew she was flipping over

Trib's right shoulder as the pony planted his front feet and ducked to the left. Christina enjoyed a second of quiet, pleasant flight before she landed hard on her side, skidded face first for a couple of feet, and came to rest with her head in a tangle of branches.

5

CHRISTINA LAY STILL FOR A MOMENT, UNABLE TO BELIEVE that she had fallen off. It was the mouthful of dirt and the bug's-eye view of the grass that forced her to admit it. She took a quick inventory of her aches and pains. Luckily the ground was soft from a week of rain. As soon as she realized she wasn't hurt too badly, she jumped to her feet. She had to catch Trib before he ran back to the barn and got everyone worried.

Her left hip throbbed where she had landed on it, but she ignored the pain and hobbled quickly around the tree stump looking for Tribbles. To her relief, she saw Kevin trotting back toward the tree, leading the pony by the reins. His anxious expression relaxed when he saw that she was on her feet.

"Chris, are you okay?" he asked.

She nodded, grinning sheepishly. "I'm fine.

Thanks for catching him," she said, gesturing toward her pony.

"It was a lucky grab," Kevin said. "When I got around the tree stump, I looked back to see how close you were, and I saw this guy come zooming up. I reached over and grabbed his reins just as he came by." Kevin looked troubled again. "You're limping. What happened? How'd you fall off?"

Christina turned around and studied the fallen tree. From the ground she could see that the section of the trunk she had meant to jump was almost up to her chest—more than three feet high, she realized. Trib couldn't have cleared it. What was she thinking? Christina started to admit her mistake to Kevin, then thought better of it. If he hadn't seen her try to jump the tree, maybe it was better not to say anything.

"He just spun left and ducked his right shoulder," Christina said, which was the truth, but not the whole truth. "And off I went. I'm okay," she assured him, though her hip still ached and her right cheek had begun to sting. She began brushing off the dirt and grass that still clung to her clothes.

"You have a big scrape on your face," Kevin observed. "It's bleeding a little."

Christina untucked her shirt and swiped at her cheek with it. It came away smeared with dirt and some blood. "Does it look very bad?" Christina asked. She didn't want to have to explain to her parents how she had fallen off.

"We should clean it," Kevin said. "It's so dirty it's hard to tell. Come on. Mount up. We'll go down to the cottage and take care of it before the parents see it and start freaking out."

Christina took the reins and climbed up on her pony. She and Kevin let the horses walk down the long slope of the hillside. By the time they had come across the pasture, both horses had cooled off from their gallop. They went a roundabout way across the property so that no one would notice them, ending up in the backyard of the McLeans' cottage.

"Is your mom home?" Christina asked.

"No," Kevin told her. "She's teaching today." His mother taught aerobics at a gym in town. "And Dad's busy at the barn. We're cool."

The cottage where the McLeans lived was a charming two-story wood house with a stone chimney climbing up one side of it. Christina held both horses while Kevin went inside. Five minutes later he was back with a pan of warm water, a washcloth, and a first-aid kit.

"C'mere," Kevin said.

Christina sat down on the back porch steps, still holding the horses, who began nibbling at the bright green grass. She tilted her face up and closed her eyes as Kevin went to work cleaning her dirty, scratched face.

"Does it hurt much?" Kevin asked, gently dabbing more warm water on her cheek.

"No," Christina lied, wincing as the water ran over the scrape. It stung horribly. She squeezed her eyes tightly closed so no tears could escape and tried to concentrate on the gentle warmth of the sun on her face.

"Chris?"

Christina opened her eyes, blinking at the bright sunlight. She touched her cheek carefully, examining the scrape with her fingers. A long welt had risen under the deepest scratch.

"Hold still," Kevin ordered her. "I'm going to put some of this antiseptic gunk on your cheek." He smeared the scrape with some gooey cream, which actually felt soothing to Christina. Then he put the cap on the tube and dumped out the water. He eyed his first-aid job critically. "It needs a Band-Aid, but it's too long for one."

"How does it look?" Christina asked.

"Not too bad," Kevin said. "But it's a good thing the spring formal is still a few weeks away," he joked.

"I hope it doesn't leave a scar," she said. "Am I going to pass the parent interrogation?"

"Maybe," Kevin said. "What are you going to tell them?"

"The truth," Christina said innocently. "You know—that we were riding and I scratched it on a tree branch."

"Right," Kevin said. "Come on. Let's put these guys away before they start eating Mom's daffodils."

He took Jasper's reins from Christina and they began leading their horses back to the stables. "Don't forget," Kevin reminded Christina, "you're buying the sodas."

That night at dinner Christina managed to convince her parents that she had scraped her cheek on a low tree branch while she was out riding with Kevin. It wasn't entirely true, but it wasn't really a lie, either, Christina reasoned. She just didn't mention that the branch was so low it was on the ground and that she had fallen off before she hit it. "It's no big deal," she said casually. "It looks much worse than it is, really," she assured them.

Then, to change the subject, she started to tell them all about riding Foster. That seemed to pique her mother's interest.

"Really? Mona let you ride Foster?" Ashleigh asked, sounding surprised.

"Yes," Christina said. "There's an Event coming up, over at Foxwood Acres. Mona says if I get along with Foster okay, I can ride him in it. If it's okay with you," Christina added hastily.

"That's great, Chris," her father said encouragingly.

Her mother frowned. "Foster's a lot of horse for you, isn't he? How'd you get along with him?" she wanted to know.

"I was a little shaky at first," Christina admitted.

54

"His trot is so bouncy compared to Trib, but once I got used to him, I was fine. And his canter is the best," Christina said. "Today I just did crossrails and a little vertical, but soon I'm going to do some bigger jumps. Mona thinks I'm ready for more height," Christina said importantly.

"Hmm," Ashleigh mused.

Christina eyed her mother. "Well, how about it? Can I go?" she persisted.

"Sure, sweetheart," Mike answered. "Okay with you, Ash?"

"Well . . ."

Christina held her breath. Her mother wouldn't really say no, would she?

Ashleigh nodded. She stood up from her chair and moved around the table to hug Christina. "My baby's really growing up," she said.

"You're not kidding," her dad said. "You'd better stop growing so fast," he joked. "If you get any taller, you'll never be a jockey like your mom."

"I don't want to be a jockey," Christina said, making a face.

"Well, how about an exercise rider or an expert trainer like your dad?"

"Dad, how am I supposed to become a trainer, or even an exercise rider, if you guys won't let me get on any of the horses?" Christina demanded.

Her parents exchanged looks. Christina knew they were thinking of the terrible fall Ashleigh had endured in her racing days—and of the Christmas Eve when Ashleigh was pregnant with Christina and had been kicked by a horse. Both Ashleigh and Christina had come dangerously close to losing their lives in that accident. That was one reason Ashleigh had been reluctant to let her daughter ride the spirited racehorse colts and fillies at Whitebrook.

"When you're a little older, dear," Ashleigh reminded her. "Anyway, you can't get your exercise rider's license until you're sixteen."

"Riding young racehorses is dangerous," Mike reminded her. "Maybe next year."

"That's what you said last year, and the year before," Christina pointed out. "At this rate I'll die of old age before I ever get a chance to risk my life on a young horse. I'm twelve years old," Christina declared. "You started riding Wonder when you were only twelve."

"That was different," Ashleigh countered. "Wonder would have died if someone hadn't taken special care of her, and no one was willing to bother with her except me. By the way, Mike, how was Legacy's work this morning? I meant to get over there to see it, but I got hung up with schooling the babies in the gate."

"Ian said it was a black letter day," Mike said with a smile.

A "black letter" workout meant that Legacy's time had been very fast. But Christina didn't care. She was annoyed at her parents for treating her like a baby. She was a good enough rider to ride Legacy and she knew it. She began arranging the asparagus spears on her plate into a jump course. The mashed potatoes made an excellent water jump with a puddle of gravy in the middle, and the roll became a hill with an Irish bank jump. Suddenly Christina realized that both her parents were staring at her. "What?" she said uneasily.

Mike laughed. "Go on and finish designing your course," he said. "It looks pretty complicated."

"We were talking about your horse, honey," her mother said. "He's really coming along well with his training. I don't like to push the two-year-olds too early in the year, but Legacy's very mature. I think he's going to be ready to race soon, so I was thinking, maybe it's time you were a little more involved with his training."

Christina's ears perked up. "Involved how?"

"Well, of course you'll need to practice on one of the older horses at first, but once you get in shape, maybe you could start exercising Legacy," Ashleigh said. "In the meantime, you can take over as Legacy's groom on weekends." She beamed at Christina as if she had just given her a huge present.

Christina managed to smile. "Um, thanks, Mom," she said, trying to sound enthusiastic. She wouldn't mind grooming Legacy, but she'd be a lot more excited if she could ride him, too, instead of practicing on some old horse first. "Can't I just start riding Legacy right away?" she pleaded.

Her mother gave her a strange, intense look, as if she were searching for something in Christina's face.

"You're not ready yet," Ashleigh said firmly after a minute.

Christina looked down for a moment, blinking to hold back tears. She knew there would be no use protesting. Her mother liked everything done in a certain order. At least riding an old racehorse would be better than nothing. "It's sort of frustrating to own a horse and not be able to ride him," she ventured.

"I imagine so," Ashleigh said sympathetically. "But it will happen soon enough, sweetheart. I just want to be sure you're ready. First thing tomorrow, we put you up on old Blue and see if you can stay on."

"Mo-om." Christina frowned. "Of course I can stay on." But impulsively, her hand went to her cheek. She had never really ridden jockey style. How would it feel to be galloping a racehorse around the training oval with her stirrups short and her head lower than her seat? Christina took a thoughtful bite of her potatoes. She guessed she would soon find out.

The next morning Christina's dad woke her just after sunrise. "Rise and shine," he sang out, tugging her by an ankle until she felt her head slide out from under her pillow.

"Da-ad," Christina groaned. "Is there some kind of law that says racehorses have to be ridden before dawn?"

"Yep," Mike said cheerfully, throwing off the covers. "So hurry it up, or we'll send the horse police out after you."

"I'm coming," Christina grumbled sleepily. Her body was slightly sore from her fall the day before but once she got out of bed and stretched to work some of the kinks out, she felt better. By the time she had grabbed a quick breakfast, pulled on her boots and chaps and made her way down to the track, she was full of energy and anxious to get started. She had to admit it was exciting to think that soon she would be galloping down the track with the dirt flying behind her, just as she'd seen Anna gallop Legacy the day before.

Her father stood waiting for her, holding Blues King. "Ready?" he asked her.

"I guess so," Christina said.

"Okay, up you go," Mike said, giving Christina a leg up.

Christina felt tiny needles of nervousness shooting through her, but she trusted Blue. The exercise saddle on the old stallion's back was slightly larger than a racing saddle. He stood patiently while Christina got her feet into the stirrups and adjusted the reins.

She put a hand on the stallion's wide neck and patted him. He arched his neck proudly and snorted under her touch. "Good boy, Blue," she said, trying to give herself confidence.

Mike had been holding the stallion steady. Now he let go and stepped back. Blue just stood there, waiting for Christina's commands. "What should I do?" she asked her father.

"Just try a little jog first and see how it goes," he suggested.

Christina nodded. A jog was the same as a trot. She could do that. The idea of riding with her stirrups so short seemed ridiculous, though. How did the jockeys stay on? Her legs seemed impossibly far above the horse's sides, and it was hard to move them, but she managed to nudge Blue with her heels and send him into a slow jog. She sat at first, then slowly stood in the irons, pushing her hips off the saddle. Immediately she felt wobbly and had to grab some mane to steady herself, but Blue seemed to realize it was her first time up. The big horse just kept jogging along slowly while Christina tried to find her balance.

"Looking good, Chrissy!" Mike called out to her as she turned around and came trotting back toward him.

Christina made a face at the hated nickname, but was too busy staying on to lecture her dad about it. At last she tugged on the reins and sat down on the saddle as Blue slowed to a walk.

Ashleigh approached Christina. She shaded her eyes from the low sun and smiled at her. "You look good up there. How do you feel?" she asked.

"Fine," Christina said, sounding more confident than she actually felt. She was still getting used to the strange position, but already she felt more secure. "Can I gallop him?" she asked.

Ashleigh looked at Mike questioningly. When he nodded, she said, "Sure, give it a try—just a slow gallop to the quarter pole, then turn around and jog back. That's probably about all your legs can take the first time. And stay off the rail," she cautioned.

Christina knew that on a racetrack, the rail was for breezing, which was much faster than galloping. Galloping horses had to stay off the rail. And jogging horses had to stay way off the rail, and go to the right, in the opposite direction from the gallopers and breezers. There were already several horses on the track. Christina noticed Anna on Legacy and waved. Then she spotted Naomi Traeger, another sixteen-year-old exercise rider at Whitebrook. Naomi was on Leap of Faith. She jogged the pretty filly over to Christina.

"Hi, Christina," Naomi said. "What're you doing up there?"

"I'm learning to be an exercise rider," Christina said. "How's Faith today?"

"She's feeling a little frisky this morning," Naomi said with a smile. The filly danced impatiently underneath her, but Naomi didn't seem concerned.

61

She handled the filly with a light, expert hand, steadying her without even stopping her conversation. "I'm just going to jog her first and take the edge off. Then when she settles we'll go for a nice, slow gallop. How's that sound, Faithy?" Naomi reached forward and stroked the filly softly. Faith looked impatient to get going, but she settled a little under Naomi's calm touch.

"She's so pretty," Christina said with admiration. Then she noticed that Naomi had the stirrups much closer to her toes than Christina did. She imitated Naomi's position as best she could, shoving her heels down deep.

"Oh, yes, she's a beauty. Aren't you, girl?" Naomi said, whispering softly to soothe the impatient filly. The girl's dark braid had fallen over one shoulder and she tossed it behind her again. Faith had begun to toss her head, anxious to get on with her exercise. "Well, we're off. Good luck with your training," Naomi said.

"Thanks," Christina answered.

"Ready to go?" Mike asked.

"Ready," Christina said. She tried to make her voice sound bold, though she felt a tiny bit afraid. Out of habit she pushed her heels down again, but they were already down as far as they would go. She turned Blue around so that he was tracking left. "Here we go," she announced and pressed her legs firmly into Blue's sides, signaling him to gallop.

The big horse sprang forward. Christina felt herself fall back and had to balance on the reins to keep from sitting down on the saddle. "Oops," she said out loud. She hadn't meant to yank on his mouth. Blue slowed when he felt pressure on the reins. Then he looked back at her, as if he were making sure she had gotten her balance. "I'm okay, Blue," she told him with a little laugh. "I'm just not used to these crazy stirrups."

In a moment she felt steady again. Blue had settled into a good working gallop, the *thrrrt, thrrrt, thrrrt* of his feet on the dirt pounding out the rhythm in Christina's ears. At first it took all her concentration to stay in the correct position, but after an eighth of a mile she had begun to relax a little. "This is more fun than I thought it would be," she said to the stallion. Too soon she was approaching the quarter pole and it was time to pull up. She tugged on the reins and felt Blue slow, then brought him down to a walk and turned him around. They jogged back to where her parents were waiting.

"You looked great, Christina," her mother told her.

"Thanks," Christina said. "It was a piece of cake." She was panting, and the muscles in her thighs trembled and burned from holding her position for so long. It was much harder than she'd thought it would be, but she figured if she didn't let on, she'd be able to ride Legacy sooner. She eased her feet out of the stirrups and let her legs dangle, grateful for the chance to stretch her thigh muscles.

"See what I mean?" Ashleigh said knowingly. "It takes conditioning. You can't jump right on and go for a mile your first time up." Christina should have known she couldn't fool her mother.

Just then Anna thundered by on Legacy. The big chestnut was flying down the track, hugging the rail, his ears cocked backward as if listening for his competition. He was majestic.

All heads turned as the colt streamed by. When they reached the quarter pole, Christina saw Anna stand up, signaling Legacy to slow down. Then she galloped him out for another furlong before easing him down to a walk.

"We're going to have to find that colt a race soon, Ash," Mike remarked. "He's ready."

"I know," Ashleigh said, gazing with approval at the big colt that Anna was now walking toward the gap.

Christina had her eye on the colt, too, but she wasn't wondering when his first race would be. She was wondering when she would be allowed to ride Legacy herself.

6

IN THE WEEKS THAT FOLLOWED THE WEATHER GREW STEADILY warmer. Soon the brilliant yellow blooms of early spring gave way to the warm pinks and whites of the blossoming dogwood and azaleas.

Every afternoon, if she didn't have too much homework, Christina got on Blue and took him for a gallop. And though she wasn't too keen on the idea at first, every weekend morning she got up when the sun was just peeking over the hilltops and went to groom Legacy.

The horse was energetic and playful when he knew he was going for a run, but in the barn he was calm and happy. At first Christina just went through the motions of grooming him, but one Saturday she began talking to him while she brushed him, and it dawned on her that she had actually begun to enjoy handling the colt. She found an itchy spot with the currycomb, and Legacy leaned into her, encouraging her to rub harder. Then he let out a series of happy little groans, which made Christina laugh. "You like that, huh?" she said, rubbing harder.

"I wish I could keep on doing this," she said to him, knocking the currycomb against a wall to get the dirt out of it. "But I've got to go now. It's time for my jump lesson. Mona says today's the day I get to jump three-six!" She put Legacy back in his stall, gave him a farewell pat, and skipped out of the barn.

Riding Foster had been one of the best things that could have happened to Christina. It wasn't the same as owning her own Event horse, of course, but it was a close second. She had finally grown accustomed to Foster's springy trot and now it didn't bother her anymore. That morning she walked him around on a long rein while she waited for Mona to adjust the height of the rail.

"All right, Chris. Canter him over this little vertical," Mona said to her after she had warmed up over some smaller jumps. "But remember," Mona cautioned, "this is set at three-six. That's going up enough in height that the horse has to make a little more of an effort to clear it. And you're going to feel that effort when he bascules—" Mona cupped her hand in a little arc to mimic the motion she was describing. "—when he rounds his back and tucks up his legs to clear the jump. Be ready," Mona said.

"I've been ready for this all my life," Christina said, smiling broadly. She circled to get an approach to the large jump. Then she cantered toward the vertical, feeling confident and relaxed.

She was ready for the takeoff. She bent forward into two-point position as the horse rocked back on his haunches and pushed off into the air. It felt just fine. Then they were in flight, all four of Foster's legs off the ground as they sailed over the vertical. But she was unprepared for the extra heave she suddenly felt as the horse tucked his feet neatly under him and rounded his back and neck. She felt herself come loose from the saddle. "Uh-oh," she said aloud, as Foster landed after the jump. It seemed like a very long way to the ground. Christina managed to come down with most of her weight in her heels, but she was a bit behind the horse's motion and had to let the reins slip through her fingers to keep from yanking his mouth.

Mona winced. "Oh, boy. That was awful," she said cheerfully.

Christina blushed. "I know. I'm sorry. Sorry, Foster," she said sincerely, giving the horse an apologetic pat.

"Christina, you can't jump a horse like this over fences this high all relaxed, like you're just doing a little equitation course," Mona instructed her. "Foster'll jump you right out of the saddle. This is a different kind of ride completely. Come at it again, now that you know what it feels like, and this time close your leg all through here," Mona demonstrated, touching her inner knee and calf. "And ride with some strength. You looked like you were taking a nap that time," Mona kidded her.

Christina smiled in spite of her embarrassment. Mona was good at getting her students to laugh at their mistakes. And she was right. Christina had been far too relaxed the first time. She got herself organized and headed for the fence again, but this time she did exactly what Mona suggested. Again she felt fine on the takeoff. In the air, she kept her calves and knees securely closed against the saddle and the horse's sides. And this time she was ready for the jarring landing. She kept her hands at the crest of Foster's neck and let her knees and ankles absorb the shock. Instantly she could tell she had done it right. Christina pulled up and patted Foster exuberantly.

"How was that?" she asked. "Better?"

Mona nodded. "A thousand times better. That's the way to ride those jumps. You feel it?"

Christina nodded emphatically. She did feel it. She knew she wouldn't make the same mistake again.

Mona had her jump the fence a few more times. Then she added another rail a couple of feet behind the first rail, making the fence more spread out, and lowered the first rail a few inches. "This is called a step oxer," she explained. "You'll have a little more time in the air, and it will feel like a little more jump

68

than the vertical. But just keep riding like you have been and you'll be fine."

A big smile broke over Christina's face as she and Foster sailed over the oxer like it was nothing. "Again?" Christina asked hopefully. She was having more fun than she could ever remember having on a horse.

Mona let them jump the oxer twice more, then said it was time to quit. Christina could have jumped all day, but she knew Foster had had enough. "I love this horse!" she told Mona, scrubbing his neck affectionately. "He is so much fun."

"You're going to do great in the Event," Mona told her.

"You think so?" Christina asked, her eyes shining.

"I know so," Mona said confidently as they trudged up the path to the barn.

Christina put Foster on crossties and untacked him. Her own saddle was too small for him, so she had been using one of Mona's saddles. She put the saddle back on its rack in the tack room and got a bucket of warm water and a sponge. She was cleaning the sweat marks off Foster's back and girth area when she realized that someone was standing near her, watching her work. She glanced up and saw that it was Dylan Becker.

"Hi," he said, smiling in a friendly way.

"Hi," Christina said shyly. She had seen him around the barn a few times in the past weeks, but she hadn't really spoken to him since the first morning she rode Foster. At school he was in her social studies class, but he sat in the back with the guys from the basketball team.

"I saw you jumping," Dylan motioned toward the ring. "You looked great."

"Thanks," Christina said, feeling hugely pleased that Dylan had noticed. She bit her lip so that she wouldn't reveal the equally huge smile that was threatening to come out.

"That oxer was about three-six, wasn't it?" Dylan observed.

"Yes," Christina said. Then she thought perhaps she should say more. "It was my first time jumping that high. It's so much fun!"

"I know. It's incredible, isn't it?" Dylan said. "I just started jumping three-six back in the fall. It makes the little stuff seem boring, doesn't it?"

Christina nodded. "The big fences are way more fun."

Dylan was silent. Christina didn't know what else to say, so she just went on scrubbing at Foster's back even though she knew it was clean.

When he didn't speak again, she glanced up to see what he was doing. He stood with his thumbs hooked casually under the top of his chaps, watching her. He caught her eye and smiled, so she smiled back at him. She was thinking that he looked really cute in the blue denim shirt he was wearing.

And he'd gotten a haircut since the last time she'd seen him. It was cropped close over his ears and in the back, and a little longer and spikier on top. She liked it.

Christina noticed Katie peering at her from down the aisle where she was grooming Seabreeze. She knew Katie was dying to know what she and Dylan were talking about. Then Christina realized she probably looked silly washing the same spot on Foster's back over and over again, so she dropped the sponge in the bucket. She was about to unclip the crossties from Foster's halter and put him away when Dylan spoke.

"Are you going to the spring formal?" he asked her.

Christina toyed with the crosstie instead of unhooking it. "Yes," she said. She usually went to school dances with a group of friends, including Katie and Kevin.

"Oh," Dylan said, glancing down. He unhooked his thumbs from his chaps, then didn't seem to know what to do with his arms, so he ended up sticking his hands in his back pockets.

"Are you?" Christina prompted him. Suddenly her heart began to pound, because she thought she knew—but didn't dare to hope—what he was going to say next.

Then he said it.

"I was wondering," Dylan said. The thumbs went

71

back in the front of his chaps. "Would you like to go to the dance with me?"

Christina froze, her hand on the crosstie clip. This was it. It had happened. Dylan Becker was asking her to the dance. She was pleased. She was amazed. She was terrified.

"Christina?" he said.

Christina swallowed hard. "Oh, yes," she managed to say.

"Good," Dylan said. He smiled at her.

She grinned back at him, then bit her lip to keep from seeming too excited.

"Well, I have to go get Dakota ready," he said.

"Oh," Christina said. Dakota was Dylan's horse.

"I'll see you around," he said, taking a step back.

Christina nodded. "See you."

Dylan started to walk away, then stopped abruptly and turned back to her. "I'll call you—can I call you?" he said.

"Sure," Christina said quickly. "Um, my number's in the book. It's under Michael Reese. At Whitebrook Farm."

"I know," Dylan said. He flashed her another warm smile and headed toward his horse's stall.

After he had gone, Christina just stood still for a moment, listening to her heart pound. Her face felt all hot and tingly and she knew she must be blushing. With trembling fingers she unclipped the crossties from Foster's halter and slowly led him back to his stall. Katie dropped the brush she was pretending to use and scurried to Christina's side.

"That was Dylan Becker you were talking to," Katie said, as if Christina hadn't realized.

"Uh-huh," Christina said softly.

"He is so cute. Don't you think he's cute?" Katie bubbled.

"Uh-huh," Christina repeated.

"Well, what was he talking to you about?" Katie quizzed her.

Christina looked at Katie and said solemnly, "He asked me to go to the spring formal with him."

"No way!" Katie said. "Dylan Becker?"

"He did," Christina insisted.

"You swear?" Katie peered skeptically out from under one raised eyebrow. "You're not just kidding me?"

Christina nodded. "I swear. He really did ask me to the dance."

Katie squealed with delight and hugged Christina, jumping up and down. "Oh, my gosh, Christina! That's great! That is so cool! Aren't you excited?"

Christina nodded again as a broad smile took over her whole face. "I still can't believe it," she said quietly. "I'm going to the spring formal with Dylan Becker."

For the rest of the day Christina was walking on air. At dinner she almost told her parents about Dylan asking her to the spring formal, but then at the last minute she changed her mind. It was still so special that she wanted to keep it to herself a while longer. She would tell them in a couple of days.

That night Christina had trouble falling asleep. When she finally did, her sleep was disturbed by strange, vivid dreams. She woke up extra early, her bedroom hazy with milky blue light.

In spite of her fitful sleep, Christina was wide awake. Moments before she had been dreaming something she struggled to bring to consciousness. She squeezed her eyes closed and tried to remember, but the dream refused to reveal itself. She opened her eyes, feeling frustrated, then crawled out of bed and stood in the bluish haze. Soundlessly she pulled on her clothes and glided down the stairs. By the back door she found her paddock boots and jacket, and after pulling them on, slipped outside.

The sun was just a promise of warmth in the dark ashes of the sky as Christina let herself into the training barn. She breathed in the familiar salty sweet smell of the horses. They greeted her with small whinnies and snorts as she made her way to Legacy's stall. The big chestnut moved to face her as she entered his stall. She hadn't turned on the lights, and she could feel him better than she could see him. She slid her hands down his neck. His coat was delicious cool silk in the soft morning air.

It was then that the dream came back to her, as if

touching the colt had brought it to life. All alone in the training barn, Christina suddenly knew with calm certainty why she had come there. She was going to ride Legacy.

The first grooms would be coming in a little while, but she had plenty of time. Some part of her recognized that what she was doing could be wrong—could be dangerous, even—but that part belonged to the daylight. She would take the colt out for a gallop in the mystical half light and be back before anyone knew.

She ran her hands over Legacy's back and found him perfectly clean. Christina didn't want anything to interrupt the perfect flow of this dream morning. Grooming him would just take time. She went to the tack room and found saddle and bridle, and in moments had the horse dressed for a ride. She led him out of his stall and he moved with a quiet compliance, as if he knew what was coming and wanted to help her. She lowered the left stirrup to mount him, then quickly adjusted them both, not jockey length, but lower.

"Let's go," she murmured. With Legacy's warm sides against her calves, she guided him out the back door of the training barn.

Outside Legacy's ears pricked forward and Christina felt him come alive. Energy surged through the colt's body like an electric current, and he shivered and tossed his head, beginning the dance down to the training oval.

"Be still," Christina told him, but she sat his jigging as if she were molded to him, and she didn't really mind it. With her legs tightly around his sides, she was secure. The colt would not shake her loose, no matter what.

The training oval spread before her, its rosy dirt track curving away into the soft mist. It had been harrowed smooth at the end of the previous day and was not yet marked by any print, horse or human. Its perfect surface looked as inviting as jumping into a still, rippleless lake.

"You want to run, don't you?" Christina whispered to the colt. She could feel him nosing toward the gap that led to the track, hungry for the river of speed that would build under his hooves as he rushed into it, over it. Christina wanted to feel it, too. She meant to take Legacy onto the track and breeze him. As Kevin would say, she had a need for speed. She was ready to ride the colt and had been for weeks, but she knew she had to prove it to her mother. Once her mother saw what she could do, maybe she'd let Christina take over as Legacy's exercise rider. She was planning to breeze the colt around the track, but when she glanced up, there was the fallen tree, lying on the hillside in a mute challenge, and suddenly Christina forgot about the track.

She rode past the gap that would have taken her into the training oval and headed instead toward the fallen tree. Legacy had been keen and willing when they were riding toward the track, but now he seemed puzzled, and balked. Christina urged him on with her legs and the colt stepped forward uncertainly. She could feel his lively energy dissolving into doubt and nervousness.

"Come on. You can do it. Get up," she whispered to Legacy. The colt obeyed her, but he was unhappy. He didn't like riding over strange territory with a rider he didn't know. Christina understood the colt's fear, but she was determined to get to the fallen tree. She was sure that once they got close, Legacy would feel the same determination she did.

Legacy balked again and tried to turn around. Again Christina sent him forward, driving the reluctant horse with her legs and seat. The horse bellowed in protest. His whole body shook with a desperate whinny that echoed shrill and hollow through the still air.

"Shush," she told him, bending forward as they went under a low branch. She skirted the edge of the woods where she and Kevin had steeplechased, and came around the trees at last to the grassy, uphill stretch.

Once more Legacy dug in his heels and tried to turn around. Christina wrestled with the reins.

The colt's eyes showed white around the corners and suddenly he panicked. He reared and tried to spin on his haunches toward the barn, but Christina was ready for him. She leaned over his neck and got him to come down. With all the strength and will she could put into her legs, Christina got the colt to trot.

In the sky over the hilltops was a slice of lemon light, and suddenly the magic time was over. For the first time Christina's resolve wavered and she began to regret bringing out the colt alone. If she turned back now, she could just put him away and no one would know that she had ever been out. But at the same time Christina realized that it was too late to turn back. Legacy didn't trust her. Right now he was obeying, but she sensed that if she let him turn toward the barn, he would be impossible to control. She had set out to prove something to herself, but now she had to prove herself to the horse as well. She bent forward, standing in the stirrups to get her weight off his back, and urged him into a grudging gallop.

"Move on," she said. Legacy was dragging his heels, making her work for every stride.

"You're a Thoroughbred," Christina said. "A racehorse. You're built to run—so run!" she shouted.

All of a sudden Christina felt something change in the colt. With the first rays of the sun glinting over the treetops and a gentle slope of sparkling grass spreading before him, Legacy regained his confidence.

Christina felt the horse kick in and begin to run

honestly, and it gave her a feeling of satisfaction. She had proven herself to him after all. The next thing she knew, she was galloping up the flat lane of grass and suddenly she wasn't riding anymore. She was flying.

Galloping on her pony when she raced with Kevin seemed like a joke compared with how fast she was going. Legacy's strides ate up the turf, blending so smoothly one into the next that Christina lost all sense of where the ground was. Never had she felt such power and speed, and it was simple and glorious and terrifying all at the same time. The wind in her face was so strong she could barely keep her eyes open, so she let them close, let the colt run.

She could have stayed there forever, but caution told her to open her eyes. The fallen tree appeared at the top of the rise before her, and though she had come up that morning intending to jump it, she realized she didn't need to anymore. That one perfect gallop had been enough. She could try the tree another day. She sank down upon the saddle and began asking the colt to come back to her.

That was when he really began to run.

Christina had thought that he was galloping flat out, but Legacy put on an extra burst of speed and tore up the last several yards toward the fallen tree. She couldn't believe how fast he was going. Desperately she hauled on one rein, trying to turn him. His head went to the side just long enough for Christina to see that he had his tongue over the bit, making it virtually useless. Then he straightened his head and leaned into her hands, dragging her at blinding speed toward the fallen tree.

Christina began to panic. She knew that Legacy was going way too fast to jump in any safe and sane manner—if he jumped at all. With a sick feeling of dread, she remembered how Trib had ducked out at the last second, sending her over his shoulder. If Legacy quit or turned, the same thing would be likely to happen. But if she came off at that speed, Christina knew she was in for more than just a scrape.

"Whoa!" she commanded hopefully. The tree loomed before them. With big branches still poking up from it, only one narrow section of the trunk was even jumpable. It wasn't any higher than the step oxer she had jumped with Foster, but at that moment it seemed the size of a giant sequoia.

Tugging on the reins with all her might, Christina made a last desperate attempt to stop the horse, and for just a second she felt his rhythm falter as he approached the tree blocking his path. But then he dug in and launched himself into the air, and Christina wrapped her fingers around his mane, closed her eyes, and hung on for dear life.

There was a moment of perfect silence as Legacy's feet stopped drumming the ground. Christina had just enough time to wonder if maybe she was going to die. Then she felt a terrible, jarring landing, and heard the pounding of Legacy's feet resume.

Christina slowly opened her eyes and realized with amazement that she was still in the saddle, still on top of Legacy. The colt, baffled by the obstacle that had suddenly appeared in his path, checked his gallop, and Christina managed to turn him around and get him to stop.

For a second, both horse and girl simply stood, one blowing, the other panting, as each struggled to make sense of what had just happened. Every muscle of Christina's body shook. At first she couldn't believe she had survived the episode. She looked herself over and couldn't find anything that seemed damaged. She peered down at the quaking, heaving horse just to assure herself that he was still underneath her and standing on all four legs. Then, unable to think what else to do, she began to laugh.

When her laughing fit was over, Christina realized that Legacy was still trembling. She reached forward and gave him a gentle pat to calm him. She was shocked that she had made it over the tree all in one piece, but it had given her an idea. If her parents wouldn't buy her an Event horse of her own, maybe she could teach Legacy to jump. Maybe he'd be better at Eventing than he was at racing. She remembered her parents talking about another horse they'd once owned, a Thoroughbred named Sierra. They had tried unsuccessfully to race the horse and then discovered that Sierra was a talented steeplechase horse. Legacy wasn't the gray mare she longed for, but maybe he would still be a good Event horse.

"Well, if you can jump it once, I guess you can do it again," Christina said. Then she picked up a trot and headed for the tree.

When Legacy had jumped it before, he'd been going too fast to stop. At the trot he had plenty of time to look at it. Christina felt Legacy's hindquarters shift back and forth uncertainly as they approached the tree. She got him to jump it, but it was a peculiar, lurching effort, and he landed on all four legs like a jackrabbit. She tried it once more with the same results. This time she noticed that Legacy didn't fold his front legs under him but stuck them straight out before him, "diving" over the obstacle. A horse that dived over fences was dangerous. Now she knew. Legacy was never going to be a jumper.

7

CHRISTINA HAD UNTACKED LEGACY AND WAS JUST ABOUT to bathe him when Anna came up to her and said, "You're wanted up at the house. I'll take him now."

A feeling of uneasiness crept into Christina's stomach as she handed over the colt. As she left the barn, she noticed some of the staff giving her strange looks. She did her best to ignore the looks and the queasiness in her stomach as she trudged up the path to the house. But when she saw her mother standing by the backyard fence waiting for her, a stern expression on her face, the feeling came back full force. Her mother must have seen the whole thing. Christina could tell she was in big trouble. Her steps slowed a little as she began running excuses through her head, trying to think of something she could say that would justify her morning adventure.

"I saw what you did out there," her mother said quietly. "I am very disappointed in you, Christina. What you did was extremely careless and dangerous."

Christina didn't say a word. She stared at the ground and tried to blink back tears. "But I'm fine, Mom," she said finally. "I didn't get hurt."

"You're lucky you didn't, but did you think about Legacy?"

"He's fine, too," Christina said uneasily. "He jumps terribly, but he didn't get hurt or anything." Her mother must know she would never, ever, knowingly hurt a horse.

"Christina, the colt is barely two years old. He's still a baby. The soft tissues in his knees haven't hardened and closed the spaces in his joints yet. Jumping a horse at this age could injure his knees severely and cause permanent damage." She looked hard at Christina, as if the words needed to be reinforced.

"I'm sorry, Mom," Christina said, tears coming out like a flood now. "I didn't know that about his knees—I didn't know it could hurt him. I wasn't really going to jump him. I just wanted to ride him. I just wanted to feel like he was mine." Her cheeks were wet as she searched her mother's face for some sign of forgiveness.

Ashleigh held out her arms and Christina ran into them. It felt so good to have her mother's warm arms encircle her. She couldn't control her crying now and her shoulders shook with sobs.

"I'm sorry, Mom," Christina said again. "I'm so sorry. I never would hurt him. You know that." Christina wiped at her eyes.

"I know, sweetheart. I know," Ashleigh crooned. "I know how much you want to ride him." She rubbed Christina's back. "Don't cry, sweetie. I know you didn't mean any harm. I can see now that I haven't been fair. I was so afraid to let you ride such big, powerful horses, but now I think it's time. You're definitely old enough to ride something bigger than a pony. Maybe we can find a way to get you more involved in Legacy's training."

"Oh, Mom, thank you," Christina said, hugging her mother hard. "I'm sorry I rode Legacy without your permission. I won't do it again. I promise."

Because school took up so much of her time, Christina started exercising Legacy on weekends. At first it was fun. The colt was as settled on the training oval as he had been wild in the pasture, and the enormous speed was thrilling. But it didn't compare with jumping Foster.

Christina began to feel more and more comfortable on Foster. Soon Mona began letting her practice jumping him on the cross-country course at Gardener Farm. It was challenging. She had to ride differently to jump up and down hillsides and across water, but Christina loved it. She was in her element cantering Foster across the grass to jump him down a steep bank, then turning to jump over a stone wall. She was having the time of her life.

Her flatwork was going well, too. She had begun putting Foster through the dressage test she would be doing in the Event at Foxwood Acres. She'd had to teach her pony the moves, but Foster knew them already. When she asked him for an extended trot or a leg yield, she usually got it right away. The big gelding still felt "heavy" in her hands sometimes, but she had learned to finesse him into doing what she asked, instead of trying to outpull him.

And then there was Dylan Becker. As he had promised, he called her, usually once or twice a week. On the phone he was funny and sincere and he always found something nice to say about her riding. In social studies class he would come by her desk and talk to her in the minute or two before the bell rang and they had to be seated.

Christina couldn't remember ever being so happy. She still wished for her own Event horse, but at least she had Foster and Legacy to ride. She was thrilled to be going to the spring formal, and she was looking forward to riding in the Event at Foxwood that same weekend. Things were going so well that Christina was completely unprepared for the news her parents gave her one night, less than two weeks before the big weekend.

She still hadn't told her parents about Dylan asking her to the spring formal, but she was planning to tell them that night. She was nibbling on a bite of chicken, trying to decide how to bring it up, when her mother spoke.

"Christina, we have some big news," Ashleigh said cheerfully.

"What?" Christina asked.

"We've found a race for Legacy. We're sending Faith and a couple of the other horses up to Belmont for a few weeks, and we've decided to bring Legacy along for the experience. There's a maiden race for two-year-olds with a nice purse. We're going to enter him in it," Ashleigh said.

"Oh, that's great, Mom," Christina said. "Where's Belmont?"

"That's the other good news," Mike said. "Belmont's in New York. We're going to make a vacation out of it, see a Broadway show, go to some fancy restaurants. You know, the whole tourist thing. Doesn't that sound like fun?"

"It sounds great!" Christina said. "You mean I get to go, too?"

"Of course," Ashleigh told her. "Legacy's your horse. You've got to be there for his first race."

"Cool!" Christina said. "When do we leave?"

"A week from Friday," Mike said. "You get to miss a whole week of school." He winked at her.

Christina dropped her fork and stared at her

parents as if they'd gone mad. They couldn't be serious.

"I can't go that week," Christina protested. "That Friday night is the spring formal at school. And it's the same weekend as the Event at Foxwood," Christina told them. "Can't we find another race for Legacy?"

Her mother shook her head. "We've decided, Christina. This is the best race for Legacy right now. I'm sorry you'll miss your Event, but there'll be others. Look at it this way—it'll give you a little more time to train, so you'll be even more prepared for the next Event."

Christina could not believe what she was hearing. Could they really make her go to New York with them? "But Mom, besides the Event, there's the spring formal. And there won't be another one of those until next year. I don't want to miss that," she argued.

Ashleigh shook her head. "Since when are you more interested in dances than horses? If this trip had come up last year you would have jumped all over a chance to go to New York."

"I have a d—" Date, Christina had started to say, but then she couldn't. "I just really want to go," she finished. "Please don't make me go to New York," she pleaded. "I can stay with Mona. She won't mind. Or with Katie. Or just leave me with Beth and Ian. Please?" Christina pleaded.

Her parents looked at each other and then back at her.

"Well, what about it, you guys? Can I stay here?"

"Sorry, sweetie," her father said. "We already got the tickets. You're coming to New York with us."

8

LATER, WHEN HER TEARS HAD FINALLY RUN OUT, CHRISTINA called Katie on the phone she had brought up to the attic with her. "Can you believe they're making me go to New York with them?" she said to Katie, her voice still ragged from crying.

"Why don't you stay with me?" Katie suggested.

"I already asked. They said no."

"Oh, Chris, that's terrible," Katie said sympathetically. "Did you talk to Dylan yet?"

"No," Christina said, feeling her heart give a lurch at the mention of his name. "I don't know how I'm going to tell him. He'll probably hate me forever. He'll probably never ask me out again," Christina said morosely.

"Yes, he will," Katie consoled her. "It's not your fault. Christina, I know you feel bad right now, but once you get to New York it'll be great. Just think—you'll be at the track the day of the race. You'll be sitting in the box with a great view. They'll announce your name on the loudspeaker when the horses are parading by."

Christina tried to get caught up in Katie's description. She sat in the old leather chair, holding the phone to her ear and trying to picture the crowds, the horses, the excitement of Belmont Park. But all she could see was Dylan and Foster.

"And Legacy will win—he's bound to!" Katie went on. "And even if he doesn't, Christina, you'll be in New York!" Katie reminded her. "The shopping will be unbelievable—I bet you won't even want to come back to Kentucky. I wish I were going to New York."

"I wish you were, too," Christina said glumly. "Instead of me."

Christina spent most of the flight to New York staring out the window at the serene landscape of white clouds and blue sky. Then she must have dozed off because she woke up to the bump of the airplane tires hitting the runway. They had landed.

Christina had barely spoken to her parents since the night they insisted she go to New York. But when she caught her first glimpse of the Manhattan skyline as the cab approached the city, she couldn't help

91

being impressed. Then she started asking questions and pretty soon she had forgotten that she was mad at them.

"Is that the Empire State Building?" Christina asked, pointing to a tall spire rising from the massive cluster of buildings.

"Yep," Mike told her. "And there's the Chrysler Building and the World Trade Center—see those two tall rectangular buildings over there?"

Christina nodded, fascinated. "Where are we staying?" she asked.

"You'll love this, Christina. The Plaza Hotel," Ashleigh told her.

"It's one of the most famous hotels in the world," Mike added. "And it's right at the south end of Central Park. I asked for a suite on the park side, so we should have a great view."

Christina felt her excitement grow. She had heard of the Plaza Hotel. The rest of the way to the city, she tried to imagine the fancy hotel, with its thick carpets and crystal chandeliers. Soon enough she didn't have to imagine it anymore because they were there. The cab pulled up in front of the grand hotel with its flags and fountain. The driver set out their bags and a bellboy swooped them onto a cart. Christina shouldered her backpack and marched into the lobby with her parents.

Just as her dad had promised, their suite overlooked Central Park. Christina dropped her backpack on the bed and stared out the window, mesmerized by the spectacular view spreading away from her. Central Park was a long rectangle of trees and lakes surrounded by buildings. A road wound its way through the park, and suddenly Christina caught sight of an old-fashioned horse-drawn carriage.

"Mom, come here. Look!" Christina called excitedly.

Ashleigh came into Christina's room and stood beside her daughter. Christina pointed to the horse and carriage. "Look at the horse and carriage. Isn't that cool?"

Ashleigh nodded. "We can take a ride in one if you like," she offered.

"Really?" Maybe this trip would turn out to be better than she had expected.

"As soon as you're ready," her father said, joining them at the window.

"I'm ready," Christina said. "Let's go."

Outside the hotel, on the street called Central Park South, there was a whole lineup of carriages for hire. Most of them were pulled by chunky draft horses wearing blinders. Christina wondered how she could have missed seeing them before.

"Which one do you like, Chrissy?" Mike asked her.

Christina moved down the line of carriages, looking at the horses. Finally she chose a white carriage with black seats, pulled by a gray draft horse with feathery plumes of hair above his enormous feet. The vases on either side of the carriage held yellow roses, and the horse's harness was trimmed with silver fittings.

A slim young woman in a white shirt and tie and formal black coat with tails was standing near the horse's shoulder. Her blond hair was gathered into a neat bun at the nape of her neck, under an elegant top hat. "Would you care to take a carriage ride today, Miss?" the young woman asked Christina.

"Can we take this one, Dad?" Christina asked.

"You're the boss," Mike told her.

"Yes, please," Christina told the young woman.

They climbed into the carriage and soon Christina found herself riding through Central Park. The driver, whose name was Leanne, pointed out the sights as they followed the winding drive north through the park. For a little while Christina sat across from her parents, listening to Leanne. Then she began to ask about the horse.

"His name's Bruno," Leanne told her. "He's a Belgian draft horse."

"He's so pretty," Christina said. She was in the backward-facing seat, just behind Leanne. She twisted around so that she could see Bruno better. His mane and tail were flowing white, and the black leather harness against his white coat looked stunning.

Leanne must have noticed her awkward position.

"Want to come sit up here?" she invited, patting the seat beside her.

"Sure," Christina said eagerly, climbing forward. Leanne scooted over and Christina settled on the driver's seat beside her. Christina was enjoying the ride and the scenery, listening to the friendly clop of Bruno's shoes on the concrete.

"So, are you on vacation?" Leanne asked her.

"Sort of," Christina said. "My parents train racehorses. We have some horses running at Belmont this week."

"Oh," Leanne said. "My uncle works on the track. He's a groom. You know the horse Studly?"

"Sure," Christina said. Studly was famous. He was the horse who had won the Kentucky Derby the year before.

"Well, my Uncle Billy is Studly's groom," Leanne explained.

Christina nodded. She was watching Leanne's gloved hands on the long driving reins, wondering how it would feel to be driving the carriage. Leanne must have noticed, because she said, "Would you like to drive?"

"Could I?" Christina said. Leanne handed over the reins and Christina took them carefully. She tried to hold them exactly as Leanne had, but as soon as she had her fingers closed around the reins, Bruno's lively walk began to falter. The big horse turned his head from one side to the other, as if he were trying to see who was driving.

Christina laughed in amazement. She didn't see how Bruno could feel all the way down those long lines that someone other than Leanne was holding the reins. "I'm doing it just like you showed me," she said. "How does he know the difference?"

"He just knows. Horses are smart." Leanne put her hands over Christina's and adjusted her hold on the reins. Then she gave the reins a shake to get Bruno going, and let Christina hold them alone again. The horse tossed his head as if he were shrugging. He gave up trying to see who was driving and trotted on. The clop-clop-clopping of his metal shoes rang out merrily and Christina realized she was having a good time. She wasn't even thinking about the Event or the spring formal anymore.

Too soon the ride was over. Christina had to hand the reins over to Leanne, who pulled up before a rambling brick-and-stone building surrounded by trees and gardens. "Here you are, folks," Leanne announced. "Tavern-on-the-Green."

Tavern-on-the-Green was a famous restaurant in Central Park. Christina's parents had told her that they were going to have dinner there. They were also going to meet her father's brother-in-law, Christina's Uncle Will, and his daughter, Melanie. Christina was curious to meet her city cousin.

The maitre d' showed them to a round table in a dining room surrounded on three sides by windows overlooking a courtyard. Christina couldn't stop staring at the intricate floral wallpaper, the cushy carpets, the lush flower arrangements, and the crystal that sparkled everywhere. "This is the fanciest restaurant I've ever seen," she said as they sat down.

The waiter was pouring ice water into the crystal goblets when Christina spotted a tall man in a stylish suit and tie looking around the dining room. He was tan and handsome, with blue eyes and shoulder-length graying hair. Christina hadn't seen him since she was a toddler, but she knew he had to be her uncle, Will Graham.

"Will," her father said at the same moment, standing up so that the man could see him.

The searching look vanished from his face and Will Graham smiled as he recognized Mike and Ashleigh. He sauntered over to the table, shook hands with Mike, and kissed Ashleigh on the cheek. Then he turned to Christina. "You must be Christina. I'm your Uncle Will," he said, offering his hand.

Christina shook it politely, noticing that he wore a narrow silver bracelet on his wrist, next to a very expensive-looking watch. He had an easy elegance about him that fascinated Christina. She had never seen a man look so comfortably stylish, and she had to try hard not to stare at him.

"Where's Melanie?" Ashleigh asked.

"She stopped off in the rest room—I think it was a hair crisis or something," he said, giving Christina a wink. "We took the convertible—here she is," he said as a girl walked up to their table. "Christina, this is your cousin Melanie."

At the first sight of her cousin, Christina's mouth almost dropped open in shock. At the last second she managed to keep it closed. "Hi," she said.

"Hi," said the girl. She was a little shorter than Christina and she wore a short dress made of several sheer layers of pastel fabric. On her feet were chunky sandals, and several different bracelets wound their way up her wrists. She had five—Christina counted them—tiny silver hoop earrings in one ear and a small diamond stud in the other. She was also wearing frosty pink lipstick. But it was the girl's hair that really held Christina's attention. It was short over her ears and long on top, and pale blond, almost white—except for the parts that had been dyed a startling shade of blue.

"Hello, Melanie," Ashleigh said warmly, giving the girl a hug. "It's nice to see you again. You were just a toddler when I saw you last." Christina knew Melanie's mother had died when she was three.

An intense expression flashed across Melanie's brown eyes as she drew back from Ashleigh's hug and sat down next to Christina. It was gone as quickly as it had come, but Christina had noticed it—anger, and maybe some sadness. Melanie's elflike face had smoothed into a sweet neutrality, but something told Christina to watch out for this girl.

The adults began to chat, catching up on each

other's lives. Christina registered snatches of the conversation as she studied her menu. Uncle Will was a producer at a big recording company. Melanie was in the seventh grade at an exclusive private school. There was a terrible leak in the ceiling of their town house that had ruined an antique carpet.

"What are you getting?" Melanie asked her.

Christina pointed to the menu. "This veal thing sounds good."

"You can't order veal!" Melanie said in disgust. The people at the table next to them stared for a few moments before going back to their meal. Christina felt her face turning red.

"Don't you know that the little baby calves are tortured?" Melanie went on. "They stay in these tiny little cages, and they get shots of hormones and antibiotics to make them grow fast just so they can be murdered." Melanie hissed the last word out.

"Melanie," Will said to his daughter. "That's enough. Christina can order whatever she wants."

"Don't you even care about the baby calves?" Melanie demanded.

"I didn't know about them," Christina said uncertainly. "Is that really true?"

Melanie nodded emphatically. "So we can't support the veal industry. It's barbaric, what they do to those poor baby animals."

"I'll order something else," Christina said, scanning the menu. But she was worried. She wondered if there was any reason why she shouldn't eat chicken.

When the waiter came to take their order, Melanie ordered a salad. "I'll have the same," Christina said.

Melanie gave her a look of approval. "I'm a vegetarian," she informed Christina and her parents.

"Melanie's very into animal rights," Will said. "However, she does ride horses," he teased.

"Riding horses is not the same as abusing them," Melanie said defensively.

"Where do you ride, Mel?" Mike asked.

"Clarebrook," Melanie said.

"It's the only stable in the whole city," Will said. "The place is tiny. I don't see how anybody can ride in there, but they do. She loves it, right, Mel? Melanie's been riding there since she was about, what, Mel? Ten? Eleven?"

Melanie studiously ignored her father. "Dad says you own a racehorse farm. Do you ride horses?" she asked Christina.

"Sure," Christina said. At least she felt safe talking about horses. If Melanie had only been riding since she was ten, Christina would be a more experienced rider. "I have a pony right now, but I would really like a horse." She emphasized the word horse and gazed meaningfully at her parents.

"Christina owns a racehorse, don't you, Chris?" Mike said, as if he hadn't heard her. "Tell them about Wonder's Legacy."

"You tell them," Christina muttered. Melanie's mouth quirked in a little smile. Apparently anything Christina said in the way of a rebuff to her parents would be looked upon favorably by Melanie.

Mike began telling Will about the horse. Christina eyed her cousin. "I like your hair," she offered. Now that she was getting used to it, she had to admit, it looked kind of cool on Melanie. "How'd you get it blue?" she asked. "Is that, like, permanent?"

Melanie shook her head. "It's Kool-Aid," she said, pulling a bright blue strand down over her eyes. "It comes out after about a week or so." She examined the strand of hair for a moment, her eyes crossing, then blew it back off her forehead. "We could do yours," she added. "It's light enough. How about red or bright orange?" she suggested. "That would look totally cool with your, um, freckles."

Christina put a protective hand to her golden-red hair. "I don't think so," she said quickly. "I don't think they'll let me." She had the uneasy feeling that there had been an insult mixed in there somewhere, but she wasn't exactly sure.

Melanie gave her a doubting look and took a sip of water. Christina spent the rest of the dinner trying to be sure she didn't say the wrong thing again. She was relieved when it was time to go.

Uncle Will and Mike both fought to pay the bill. Christina didn't even notice who won. When they got up to leave the restaurant it was about seven-thirty and daylight was beginning to fade. They stood in the courtyard outside the dining room, the adults discussing when to get together next. The courtyard was surrounded by topiary trees and bushes trimmed into animal shapes. There were Japanese lanterns strung overhead, and the biggest trees were wrapped with what had to be millions of tiny white lights, all the way to the ends of the smallest branches. Christina could imagine how pretty it would look in the dark.

The familiar sound of horses trotting reached her ears, and a second later Christina saw two riders on a wide dirt path just beyond the courtyard. A handsome, dark-haired young man was leading, riding an equally handsome dun horse with a dark dorsal stripe. Behind him was an anxious-looking, middle-aged woman on a tired-looking, stiff-legged Appaloosa lightly splotched with gray. The young man looked as happy and at ease as the woman was tense.

Melanie's face lit up. "Hi, Jonathan," she called, waving at the riders. "How's Brutus?"

"You know him?" Christina asked.

"Yeah, that's my riding teacher," Melanie said airily. "Jonathan Kelly. He's the best."

The young man slowed his horse, peering into the courtyard. Then he smiled and waved back. "Melanie, hello! Brutus is a little fussy today!" he reported as the dun horse tossed its head, annoyed at being held back. He glanced behind him and spoke to his student. "Heels down, Ms. Roberts," he admonished. Then he cantered off, the woman following behind.

"Bye, Jonathan!" Melanie yelled after him.

"Can anybody ride in the park?" Christina asked.

"Well, not anybody," Melanie said. "You have to know what you're doing."

"Hey, that's a great idea," Uncle Will said as they strolled to the front door of the restaurant. "Maybe you two could go for a ride in the park tomorrow."

"That would be nice," Christina said hopefully.

"You'll show your cousin around the bridle path, won't you, Mel?" Uncle Will said cheerfully.

"Sure thing, cuz," Melanie said. But Christina thought there was something devious about the way she said it.

"We'll set it up tonight," Will promised. He glanced at his watch. "I have to run," he said, his friendly expression instantly becoming smooth and businesslike. "Come on, Mel. I'll drop you at the house."

"I thought you were going to be home tonight," Melanie said to her father. For the first time, Christina detected something in Melanie's tone that wasn't purely tough and challenging.

"I can't help it, Mel. This meeting has been rescheduled four times. You know how unpredictable musicians are. I have to see these guys tonight. Let's go, sweetheart. Good night, everybody," Uncle Will said.

"See ya later, Country Mouse," Melanie said to Christina, and followed her father toward the parking lot.

The next morning Christina's parents took her to Clarebrook Stables. Behind the front desk in the little office was a harried-looking but friendly young woman who checked them in and told Christina to fill out a release form, giving her permission to ride Clarebrook horses. Ashleigh signed the form and paid for Christina to ride.

"All right, Chris," Ashleigh said. "We're heading to Belmont to make sure the horses arrived all right and help get them settled in. We'll be back to pick you up this afternoon, okay? If you need to reach us, here's the number for the barn office at Belmont." Ashleigh handed Christina a slip of paper with a number on it. "Whoever answers should be able to track us down."

"Melanie's not here yet," Mike said worriedly. "Will you be okay?"

"I'll be fine, Dad," Christina said, rolling her eyes.

"Don't go out of the stable by yourself, you hear?" her father cautioned her. "This is a big city and you don't know the neighborhood."

"Yes, Dad, I know," Christina said. "I promise I

won't go anywhere without Melanie. Just go, will you?" The office was starting to fill up with people ready for the first rides of the day.

"Bye, sweetie," he said. "Have a great time."

"Bye," Christina said to her parents.

When they had finally gone, she sat down in the office to wait for Melanie. While she was waiting, Christina gazed out into the ring. It was hard to believe that people could actually ride in such a tiny space. The riding arena was really just the main floor of the building, with dirt footing laid down for the horses to travel on. And there were two rows of metal poles down the middle of the ring, holding up the ceiling. The riders had to steer around them. Christina was amazed that no one bumped into them.

The horses lived on the floors above and below, with ramps to get up and down instead of stairs. Christina watched a horse with interest as it made its way carefully down the ramp from upstairs. Then she studied the horses already in the ring. Some of them were typical, funny-looking, lumpy old school horses. Others were sleek and handsome. She saw one rangy old chestnut that had to be a Thoroughbred. The woman adjusting his tack tightened the girth too fast and the horse bit her right in the seat. Christina stifled a giggle. One girl a little younger than Christina was trotting around on a handsome black-and-white spotted Appaloosa. He

105

looked old, but Christina bet that in his younger days he had been quite beautiful.

She was just wondering what horse she would be riding when Melanie finally appeared. "Hi, cuz," Melanie chirped.

"Hi," Christina said, unable to keep from eyeing Melanie's outfit.

Over her jeans Melanie was wearing a pair of lavender suede chaps with dark purple fringes. Christina had never seen chaps that color. They were certainly not traditional, but Christina thought they were actually kind of pretty. Her own chaps were just plain brown.

"Ready to go?" Melanie asked.

"Yep," Christina said, putting on her safety helmet and snapping the harness under her chin.

Melanie strolled over to the desk. "Hi, Jaylaan," she said to the pleasant young woman who had taken the release form. "This is Christina, my cousin from Kentucky."

"Nice meeting you, Christina," Jaylaan said. To Melanie she said, "Are you guys going to the park?"

Melanie nodded. "Can I take Milky Way?"

Jaylaan studied the appointment book before her. "That's fine. And who do you want your cousin to ride?" Jaylaan peered over the top of the desk at Christina. "What kind of rider are you?" she asked.

"I have ridden English since I was little, and I have a pony," Christina said. Out of the corner of her eye she saw Melanie mimic her words with a bratty face.

Jaylaan ignored Melanie. "What's your pony like?" she asked.

Christina smiled, thinking of Trib. "Well, he's kind of a wild man sometimes, but he can be really good. I've done the pony hunters with him, and some jumpers. But lately I've been riding my trainer's horse. I'm an Event rider," Christina said. That wasn't quite true, since she hadn't actually done an Event yet, but Christina figured it was close enough to describing the kind of rider she was. She saw Melanie watching her coolly as she explained her experience to Jaylaan.

"Cool. How high do you jump?" Jaylaan asked.

"Three-six," Christina told her.

Melanie's eyebrows shot up, revealing a second of surprise, before her expression became neutral again. "She's really good, Jaylaan," Melanie said. "Give her somebody fun. How about Kenwood?" Melanie said, smiling sweetly at Christina.

Jaylaan looked skeptical. "Are you sure?"

"Sure—she can handle him. He bucks a little, Christina. You're okay with that, right?" Melanie said confidently.

"Oh, sure. A little bucking doesn't bother me," Christina assured them.

"Kenwood's one of the nicest horses in the barn. He's got this great canter," Melanie said.

"Have you ridden him, Melanie?" Jaylaan asked.

"Not in the park," Melanie admitted. "But I've ridden him inside. Christina can handle him."

Jaylaan shrugged. "Okay then—take Kenwood," she said to Christina.

"Come on, Country Mouse," Melanie said, pulling Christina by the arm. "I'll show you where to wait."

Christina frowned at the nickname. She knew Melanie was making fun of her, but she decided to let it slide, and followed Melanie into the ring. Melanie's horse came from upstairs, and Kenwood lived downstairs, so the girls were waiting at different ramps. Christina waited behind two other women. They were discussing the horses they were going to ride in the park that morning. Christina listened with interest.

"I'm taking Bach today," one of the women was saying. "Who are you riding?"

"Oh, I'm sticking with Lorenzo," the other woman replied. "He's my favorite. I love Milky Way, too, but they say he's reserved for beginning riders in the park. It's such a shame, because I used to really enjoy him."

"You should try Bach sometime," the first woman said. "He's great."

"Oh, not for me," the Lorenzo rider said. "I heard that Bach is a real bucker in the park."

"Really?" the first woman said. "I've had him out before and he's never bucked. But once I took out this

108

horse who spooked at a bicycle and started bucking like crazy. Then he ran away with me."

"They should get rid of horses like that," the other woman said.

"Well, I usually don't mind a bit of a challenge," the Bach rider went on, "but that horse was a maniac. I don't know how I stayed on. Luckily I got him to stop before he ran into the street with me."

"Remind me never to ride that one. What was its name?"

"Kenwood."

Christina caught her breath. That sneaky Melanie.

As the women went to get their horses, Melanie approached Christina leading a chocolate brown Appaloosa with nougat-colored spots. Christina was about to shout at her cousin for requesting such a wild horse for her, but then the groom called out, "Kenwood," from the bottom of the ramp, and a big, handsome chestnut with two hind socks and a crooked white stripe down his nose came scrambling into the oval. Christina caught him by the reins and led him into the middle of the ring. She had to spend nearly half a day with Melanie, and this was Melanie's turf. If she confronted her cousin now, it could be a miserable few hours until her parents came back. Christina looked into the horse's brown eyes. He peered gamely back at her through his chestnut forelock, which fell rakishly over one eye. Suddenly Christina knew that Melanie was challenging her in a way. She was ready to take the challenge.

She unbuckled Kenwood's girth and repositioned the saddle. When she had the girth tightened, she mounted the horse and looked around for her cousin.

"Ready, Mouse?" Melanie called to her. She was walking the Appaloosa around the track.

Christina nodded. She took a deep breath and followed Melanie out the door.

They had to ride through the streets for a couple of blocks to get to Central Park. Christina was alert for whatever pranks Kenwood might try with her, but he marched steadily forward, unfazed by the taxis zooming by them. At Central Park West they had to wait for the traffic light to change. Then they rode into the park and Christina heard the sounds of the cars fade behind them, replaced by the rustle of tree leaves and the rubbery footfall of the joggers who streamed by. An in-line skater zipped by, darting between her and Milky Way, and Kenwood tossed his head and pranced a little. Christina tugged on the reins, though, and he settled right down.

"This is the bridle path," Melanie informed her as they headed down a wide dirt path. The path circled a wide, sparkling reservoir of blue water, enclosed by a high cyclone fence. The two girls began following the path around it.

"Want to trot?" Melanie asked.

In answer, Christina pushed her legs into

Kenwood's sides, asking the horse to trot on. Milky Way joined him, and the two horses trotted side by side along the path. Further ahead, Christina glimpsed a row of trees heavy with pink blossoms.

"What kind of trees are those?" Christina asked.

"Cherry," Melanie answered.

"They're pretty," Christina remarked.

So far Kenwood hadn't done anything that would make her think he was up to no good. Christina thought he seemed well mannered and pleasantly forward-going. She began to think that maybe the two women who'd been talking about him just weren't very good riders. She was glad she hadn't said anything to Melanie after all. She would have just sounded like a scaredy-cat whiner.

The wind skimmed the surface of the reservoir and tickled the cherry blossoms, sending down a scattering of pink petals. "Here's the Fifth Avenue stretch. The footing's pretty good here. Want to canter?" Melanie asked.

"Sure," Christina replied. She asked Kenwood to canter, and he started off smoothly. Five strides into his canter she knew she was going to enjoy him. They had come around a bend and were now cantering along the stretch of bridle path lined with cherry trees. The wind shook the blossom-loaded boughs overhead as the girls rode by, and suddenly they were cantering through a delicate rain of swirling cherry petals. Christina caught Melanie's eye and smiled. She was having fun. Melanie even smiled back.

Then, from out of nowhere, a dog appeared trailing a leash—a small terrier just stupid enough to take on a fifteen-hundred-pound opponent. The terrier began barking ferociously and headed straight for the two horses. At first Christina was afraid the dog would be kicked or trampled, because it began snarling and biting at Kenwood's heels. Then she realized that that wasn't going to happen, because Kenwood grabbed the bit in a rein-wrenching hold and started to run.

The cherry trees became a pink-and-brown blur as they sped past. Christina saw people scatter right and left as Kenwood thundered up the bridle path. Christina was trying to get Kenwood's mind off running by jerking hard on one rein. She was hoping to get his head up and to the side, so she could turn him and slow him down. But when he felt the bit slam into his mouth, Kenwood began a series of masterful bucks, rounding his back rigidly underneath her and plunging hard toward the ground with each buck like some kind of evil dolphin. Christina managed to keep her stirrups somehow. She braced back against his bucks, still tugging on one rein as hard as she could. The name of the game was stay back. If he got her to lean forward even a little, she knew he would buck her off.

The horse began lurching sideways, and Christina

gritted her teeth and stayed with him. Something about the motion seemed familiar, and she realized he was behaving like a larger, meaner version of Trib. Then Christina knew she had him. Kenwood gave up the bucks and put all his energy into bolting for home, but Christina was ready for him. Timing it just right, she released the rein contact on one side, then gave a series of rapid, hard jerks on the rein, designed to get the horse's head up and turn him to one side.

It worked. Kenwood's head flew up in dismay, scattering flecks of foam. He checked his bolt, and in a few seconds Christina had him stopped. He stood still, panting, and looking slightly baffled, as if he'd never come this far with a human still attached to his back.

Some of the people walking on the bridle path began to applaud. "Go, cowgirl!" one guy yelled at her.

A cute teenage boy stopped to talk to her. "Are you okay?" he asked. Christina nodded. "That was beautiful. Man, you can really ride," he said admiringly.

"Thanks," Christina said, grinning shyly.

The boy kept smiling over his shoulder at her as he walked away. "Beautiful!" he called back to her.

Christina was feeling proud of herself. Kenwood had behaved worse than any horse Christina had ever sat on, and she had ridden through it. She heard footsteps behind her, and when she looked back she saw Melanie trotting up on Milky Way.

"Hey, Mouse, that was some awesome riding!" Melanie said excitedly. "How'd you stay on?"

Suddenly Christina was as angry as she'd ever been. She whirled Kenwood around to face her cousin. "What'd you do that for?" she demanded.

"What do you mean?" Melanie said innocently. "I didn't make the dog chase you."

"You know what I'm talking about," Christina said icily. "I heard some people talking about Kenwood when I was waiting for him to come up the ramp. You wanted me to fall off, didn't you?"

"Of course not," Melanie protested. "Why would I do that? I'd just get myself in trouble."

Christina thought she sounded sincere, but she couldn't be sure. She was sure of one thing, though: She didn't trust Melanie at all.

"I wouldn't want my Country Mouse cousin to get squashed by a big city horse," Melanie gushed.

Christina glared at her. "Stop calling me that," she said firmly.

"What?"

"You know what. I'm not a mouse. I think I just proved that," Christina said, gathering up Kenwood's reins. "I don't see you riding Kenwood. In fact, I notice you chose a nice safe beginner horse for yourself," she said. It was the only insult she could think of at the moment, but it had the effect she desired.

Melanie's face turned almost the color of her chaps. "You're just a hick from Kentucky," she spluttered. " 'I have a pony' and 'I have a racehorse' and 'I can jump three-six,'" Melanie said in a sarcastic imitation of a bratty child. "With your perfect mother and father. La, la, la. You think you're going to impress anybody with that crap? You don't know anything!"

"I know I'm not a spoiled rotten city kid who would risk getting somebody injured just because she's jealous!" Christina said.

Melanie's face looked like a storm cloud. Christina waited for whatever the next insult would be. To her surprise, Melanie suddenly burst out laughing. Christina felt her own anger dissolve into confusion. What was so funny?

"Come on," Melanie said at last. "Christina," she added. "It's time to head back."

Without another word between them, the girls trotted the rest of the way around the reservoir. Kenwood was a perfect gentleman the rest of the ride. Christina had the feeling that she'd passed some kind of test, not only with Kenwood, but with Melanie. Melanie's remark about Christina's parents kept bothering her. How could Melanie blame Christina for having two parents? She knew that Melanie only had her father, but Uncle Will seemed like a nice enough guy. She decided that Melanie was just spoiled and jealous. Obviously Melanie had been playing some kind of game with her, setting her up to fail. For a while Christina felt as if she'd won the game, whatever it was. But once on the way back she caught a glimpse of Melanie's face as they turned a corner. She could have sworn Melanie had tears in her eyes, and then Christina wasn't so sure she'd won anything at all.

9

CHRISTINA'S MOTHER WOKE HER VERY EARLY THE NEXT morning. They were all going out to Belmont. Christina went to the window and pushed the curtain aside. She saw that the whole city was slick with misty drizzle. Fog lay over the trees in the park, and past a certain distance, the buildings simply vanished in the thick white mist.

Christina had watched the weather report the night before. Back in Kentucky the sun was shining. Katie and Dylan would be on their way to the Event at Foxwood. If she weren't stuck in this dreary city with her parents and her mean cousin, she'd be going to the Event with them. Slowly Christina let the curtain fall back across the window. She had been doing her best not to think about missing the Event and the dance, but now she couldn't get her mind off it. She knew there would be other Events to compete in, but she wondered if there would be any more dates with Dylan. He had said he understood when she told him that she couldn't go to the dance with him, but she still felt awful about missing her first real date ever. The drizzly gray weather made her mood official—she was miserable.

Her father had called a car service to take them to the track. Christina slumped in the back seat of the sedan, listening to the tires hissing on the wet road. When the driver stopped at the back gate of Belmont, she got out of the car and wordlessly slammed the door. Then she glumly followed her parents down a misty, tree-lined lane toward a group of barns.

"This is our barn—number seven," her father told her, pointing to the number painted in blue on the outside of the building. "All the barns look alike at first, so remember the number," he cautioned her. "This place takes up four hundred thirty acres, so you can get pretty lost if you don't know your way around."

Her mother had gone to the track to check on the horses that were already out getting their exercise. Mike showed Christina around the barn, chattering about prerace training strategy and the advantages of feeding a horse after his workout instead of before it.

Ian McLean had stayed at Whitebrook, and his assistant trainer, Maureen Allegretti, had come to oversee the horses they'd brought to Belmont. They had selected five horses besides Legacy: Leap of Faith was starting out her four-year-old season with an allowance race. Shining's roan colt, Shining Moment, and a black filly called Matilda, were each entered in a race for three-year-olds. Saturday Affair, a six-year-old chestnut gelding, jointly owned by Maureen and the Reeses, was running in a stakes race. And there was one colt for sale, sired by The Terminator, out of an unraced mare from an excellent line. The colt, Arnold's Boy, had proven himself by winning two races as a two-year-old, but he was becoming difficult to handle. Mike didn't want to geld him because of his potential as a stud, but he also didn't have room for another stallion. So they planned to enter Arnold in a $17,000 claiming race.

At last Christina had heard enough about racing strategy. "Can I go for a walk around by myself, Dad?" she asked.

"Sure, sweetheart," Mike said. "Just don't get lost. I'm going over to the track. If you need to find me, it's right over there," he said, pointing. "Just follow that road. I'll be near the clockers' house."

Christina meandered down to the end of the barn. What she really wanted to do was find a cozy hiding place somewhere, maybe behind a convenient stack of straw bales, where she could sit and be properly miserable for a while. But where was the straw stored? She followed the aisle around a turn and saw

119

what she was looking for: a stall stacked high with bales of golden straw.

She had just climbed halfway up the stack and was about to nestle herself into the dim space between two bales when she heard a commotion in the aisle. She peeked around the stall wall and saw a short, grubby-looking man with a dark face and dark eyes leading a horse.

It looked more as if the horse was leading him, though. The horse fought the groom every step, sometimes balking, forcing him to pull hard on the lead shank and sometimes charging ahead until the shank across its nose forced it to stop. Christina sensed that the man was afraid of the horse and surely the horse feared him. A horse with nothing to fear from a man would move quietly along with him when being led. This horse was showing fear—but what the man showed the horse was his anger.

He and the horse fought each other all the way down the aisle, until they reached the stall next to where Christina was hiding. She jerked her head back so she wouldn't be seen and pressed her ear against the boards that separated the two stalls. She heard the man cursing at the horse. He had a foreign accent that she couldn't identify. Then she heard a muffled smack and the horse's squeal followed rapidly by the sound of two metal shoes hitting the wall. The stall door closed with a violent slam and she heard the groom muttering angrily as he walked away. When she thought he was gone, she peeked slowly around the edge of the stall.

The aisle was empty. Christina climbed down from the straw and cautiously peered into the stall through a crack in the boards. What she saw made her gasp.

In the stall was the most beautiful gray mare Christina had ever seen. The mare's coat was a masterpiece of dark dapples, and her mane and tail were black, vividly streaked with silver. She was tall for a Thoroughbred. Christina guessed her height at about sixteen hands.

The mare stood in the corner, her head down, trembling. Christina sensed that something was wrong. She'd seen enough horses to recognize one in pain. "What's wrong, beautiful?" she said softly.

The mare turned her drooping head toward the sound of Christina's voice, and Christina was instantly charmed by her beautiful dark face and eyes. But the troubled expression on the mare's face made Christina's heart ache.

"What's the matter, pretty girl?" Christina murmured. Then she thought she caught a glimpse of a lump on the mare's neck. Christina tried looking through another crack, but couldn't get a good view. Frustrated, she stood back and surveyed the door. Like most stall doors, the top half could be opened for the horse to see out and socialize, while the bottom door kept the horse enclosed. Usually the top door would be left open. Why was this horse all shut up?

With a glance up the aisle to be sure no one was around, Christina put a hand on the top door latch and slid it open. When the mare heard the top door open, she flinched and faced the corner again. Christina saw her shift her hind legs nervously.

"What's the matter, girl?" Christina said. "I won't hurt you. Come here and let me see your neck."

The mare looked back at Christina. Then slowly she shifted around until she was facing her. Christina could see a welt the size of her hand on the horse's otherwise perfect neck. She thought about what she'd heard from her hiding place in the stall next door. She realized that the surly groom must have hit the horse. "Oh, you poor thing," Christina whispered.

The mare's ears flicked forward, back in fear, then forward again, as Christina spoke in a low voice, inviting the mare to come closer. Finally the ears stayed forward. The mare took one step, then another. Christina slowly put out a hand. The mare drew in a nervous breath, her nostrils flaring as she debated whether to keep coming or turn away. Christina didn't move. Tentatively, the mare took the last step forward. Christina felt the velvet muzzle and the rush of warm breath upon her hand. The mare's dark eyes were full of questions. Could she trust this human? Christina could see that she wanted to. She held still, giving the mare a chance to accept her. In another second she would be able to stroke the dappled forehead. Then she could get a closer look at that ugly mark on the mare's neck.

"Hey, girl, get away from there!"

Christina felt her heart nearly jump out of her chest. The mare's ears went instantly flat against her head and she made a vicious snap. Christina snatched her hand away just in time. The mare turned her back again and ran into the corner of her stall.

Guiltily Christina backed away from the door. The groom she'd seen before was coming toward her, waving his arms in a gesture that Christina guessed was meant to reinforce his words.

"You stay away from that horse! She no good!" the groom said.

"I'm sorry," Christina said. "I didn't mean any harm." She decided to play dumb. "I . . . I just wanted to pet her."

The groom gave an evil-sounding chuckle. "You pet that one, she bite off your hand," he said, baring a set of crooked yellow teeth in imitation of a horse biting. Actually his teeth looked scarier than the horse's, Christina thought. She had never disliked anyone on first sight, but something about this man completely repelled her. Unconsciously she inched away from him.

"She's so pretty," Christina said, still pretending to

be some dopey horse-crazy kid. "How come she bites?"

"She pretty, she bad," the groom grumbled. He started to close the top door. The horse suddenly wheeled around and charged at the groom, just like The Terminator did back at Whitebrook. The groom slammed the stall door in the horse's face and closed the latch. Christina winced as she heard the door hit the mare's nose.

"Don't hurt her," Christina begged.

"Huh," the man scoffed. "You see her? You see she come after me? She no good." He shook his head. "You stay away, you hear?" He warned her. He wasn't much taller than Christina, but he drew himself up menacingly, like a snake puffing up to frighten away a bigger animal. "You stay away!"

Christina had had enough. The man was scaring her as much as he'd scared the horse. Without a word, she turned and ran. As she rounded the corner, the man's unkind laughter followed her back around the end of the barn to the safety of barn number seven.

Christina decided this was no time to wait and see what happened next. The beautiful gray mare was obviously being abused. She would go straight to her parents and tell them what had happened. They would know what to do.

Remembering her father's directions, Christina followed the lane that led up to the training track.

Halfway down the stretch on one side she spotted the clockers' house and she began running toward it as fast as she could.

The clockers' house was a small wood-frame building overlooking the track with an upstairs floor where the clockers sat with stopwatches timing the workouts of the horses. It seemed to take forever, but at last Christina reached the little house and dashed inside. In the ground-floor room were a couple of exercise riders watching through the windows that lined the wall facing the track. Christina went to the first one—a tall, skinny girl with a long ponytail. "Have you seen my father, Mike Reese?" Christina asked urgently.

"Mike Reese?" She shook her head. "Don't know him. Hey, Brenda, you know Mike Reese?" she asked the other girl.

Neither of them did. Christina thought of the beautiful gray horse alone and helpless in the barn with the abusive groom. She had to help her! Christina looked around impatiently and spotted the staircase that led to the second floor. She ran up the rickety stairs and stood panting as she searched the room.

There were three or four guys with logbooks and stopwatches clocking the workouts. In fact, Christina noticed, they each had two stopwatches, so they could time more than one workout at once. They chatted easily with each other, all the while keeping up with which horse was being timed on which watch. Then Christina spotted her father, standing by the clocker in the corner.

"Dad!" she said, rushing over to him.

"Hey, Chris," he said jovially. "Boys, this is my daughter, Christina. Christina's the official owner of Wonder's Legacy."

"Hello, Christina," the clocker beside her dad said.

"Hi," Christina said politely. "Dad, I—"

"Just a minute, sweetie," Mike said.

Christina waited impatiently. The groom could be hurting the gray mare while they were standing there.

"He's going to do a mile," Mike was saying to the clocker. "You got him? The chestnut with the four white socks and the blaze."

"I got him," the burly clocker said, punching the button with his thumb.

Christina tried again. "Dad, there's something I—"

"There he goes. Christina look! There goes your horse. Watch now," Mike said, moving over to put an arm around Christina's shoulders and pull her toward the window where she could get a better view.

Christina thought she was going to scream. This was no time to watch a stupid workout. The gray mare was in danger. "Dad!" Christina said urgently. "I have to talk to you."

"Just a minute, Chris," he said again, his eyes glued to the horse now rounding the turn.

Frustrated, Christina watched, too. Legacy roared down the stretch. As he passed under the wire, the clocker punched the button.

"What'd you get?" Mike asked. He kept his voice low and even, but Christina knew her father well enough to read the excitement in his tone.

"Two-oh-three," the clocker said, logging the time in his notebook. Christina knew that meant two minutes and three tenths of a second. She also knew it was pretty fast. "What'd you get, Chuck?"

"I got him at two-oh-two," the other clocker replied.

"That's a mighty nice colt you have there, Miss," the first clocker added.

Her father squeezed her shoulders with one strong arm. "Thanks, boys. See you around," he said. Then he let Christina pull him by the hand back down the stairs and out the door.

Outside the clockers' house, Christina stopped her father. "Dad, listen," she said, and told him about the gray horse and the groom.

He listened carefully to the story. Then he took her by the shoulders and looked her in the eyes. "Chris," he said. "Listen to me carefully. We run a safe, professional training facility. Most people do, but there are a few bad folks out there. If you ran across one of them today, the best thing you can do is just be sure you don't cross his path again. Do you understand me?" His normally kind, happy blue eyes were intense and full of warning. "Don't mess with guys like that."

"But, Dad, the horse was hurt!" Christina wailed. "I know he hit it! And he'll do it again. There must be something we can do to protect the horse."

Mike shook his head. "There are no rules for how a groom has to handle his charges. If the horse is vicious, and it sounds like she is, the groom is wise to be on his toes with her. And if she is vicious," Mike said pointedly, "it's all the more reason for you to stay away from her."

"But, Dad." Christina was nearly crying now. "She's so beautiful, and he hurts her—I know he does. She doesn't deserve it! No animal does!"

Mike sighed. "Did you actually see the groom hit the horse?"

Christina shook her head. "But I heard it. I heard him smack her, and she squealed and kicked at him."

"Chris, if you didn't see it, you can't be sure what happened. How do you know the mare didn't bite or kick at him first?" Mike asked.

Christina scuffed at the dirt with one toe. "I did see him slam the door in her face," she remembered.

"Maybe he was just trying to get away," Mike pointed out. "It sounds like she's an ill-tempered mare with a tough groom, the best kind of groom for a horse that bites and kicks. There are lots of different ways of handling horses, Chris."

"I know that, Dad," Christina said. "But I know what was going on in that stall. That horse was hurt."

Her father made it clear she should stay away from the gray mare, but Christina knew she couldn't. If her father wouldn't help her, she'd just have to help the horse herself.

Christina wasn't exactly sure what she was going to do, but she knew she had to do something. The mare's dark eyes held a silent appeal for help. In spite of her fear and pain, the mare had trusted Christina, and Christina had silently promised the mare that she wouldn't let her down. Now she had to find a way to keep that promise.

"If they won't believe me, I'll just have to get proof somehow," Christina muttered to herself as she stalked back toward the barn. But how? Both her father and the groom had warned her to stay away from the horse. She couldn't risk going back into the aisle where the mare was stabled.

She was standing in the Whitebrook aisle, hands on her hips, trying to think what to do, when a barn swallow swooped down from the rafters above and out the door. She looked up and saw a scraggly swallow's nest of mud and straw tucked into the angle where a joist supported a beam. That gave her an idea. She hurried down the aisle to the stall she judged would be back-to-back with the gray mare's stall on the other side of the barn. It was Matilda's stall, but the filly was out being exercised. Christina found hand- and toeholds in the boards and managed to climb up the stall wall until she could stand on the edge of the topmost board. Then she stood on it and climbed onto the hefty crossbeam that ran the width of the barn.

Perched on the foot-wide beam, Christina began to move along it, heading toward the other side of the barn. It was dusty up there, and her hands and knees sent down little showers of dust mixed with hay. Here and there were old, empty swallow's nests covered with bird droppings. Christina crawled carefully along the beam, waving the cobwebs out of her way and avoiding the bird poop, until she had crossed the width of Matilda's stall. Now came the tricky part. She had to crawl around a joist that connected the beam to the ceiling overhead. She stood up slowly, hugging the rough joist, then shifted her weight carefully until she had stepped around it. Now she was exactly in the middle of the beam, in the V formed by the two joists, with a good view of the gray mare's stall below her. She made herself as comfortable as she could and settled down to wait for the groom to appear.

She sat on the beam for what must have been over an hour judging by the numbness in her arms and legs. She had shifted herself to every position possible, and had been through each position three

130

times by then, and still nothing had happened. The mare below her munched hay and dozed on her feet, behaving like a normal horse.

Suddenly there was the sound of whistling and footsteps coming down the aisle. Christina almost rolled off her perch and had to catch herself by grabbing the beam between her knees. It was the groom.

The mare was instantly alert. Her ears twitched back, her head jerked up, and she began pacing around the stall. Christina watched how the horse went from calm to anxious as soon as she heard the groom approaching and felt her own heart begin to pound with anxiety.

Then the latches on the stall door slid back, and the groom opened the door and entered. The mare reacted by running headfirst into a corner where she could defend herself with her hindquarters. The groom muttered something in another language. Then he spoke to the mare in English. "Come on, you witch," he said. "You got a race today."

He was holding a cheap blue nylon halter with a chain lead shank attached. He started cautiously toward the mare's left shoulder. From her perch above, Christina saw the mare's eyes look back in terror. Then she shifted her hindquarters to the left, blocking the groom's approach. He backed off and moved around to the other side. The mare made the same response, and the groom swore softly, but he kept coming toward the horse. That was when Christina saw him reach under his pant leg and pull something from his boot.

Christina's view was blocked by the joist. Desperate to see better, she shifted her hold and leaned over a little. She almost slipped, and had to grab the joist with both arms, disturbing the thick dust. The gray sprinkles began to rain down into the stall. Christina held her breath. Would the groom see the dust and look up? Luckily he was too involved with the horse and didn't notice. Then Christina saw what he had taken from his boot, hidden under his pant leg. It was a thick stick, about eighteen inches long—just the right size to raise a big welt on the neck of a horse. He held it up where the mare could see it and waved it menacingly.

The mare cowered, shrinking away from him. In one quick move, he threw the lead shank around her neck and held it tight around her throat, with the same hand that held the stick. With the other hand he pulled the halter roughly over her head. The mare closed her eyes and cringed as he adjusted the buckle and slipped the chain over her nose. Christina understood the mare's fear. Involuntarily, Christina closed her own eyes. Then suddenly she opened them wide. She was about to sneeze!

She clapped both hands over her nose and mouth and held her breath, willing herself to hold back the sneeze. The groom was wrestling with the mare, who was refusing to be led out of her stall. She planted her front feet firmly and resisted the groom's efforts to muscle her out the door. Christina relaxed the hand over her mouth and nose as the impulse to sneeze passed.

Whatever small amount of patience the groom had, was long gone. He shouted at the mare to get out of the stall. To her horror, Christina saw the groom raise the stick and begin beating the mare's shoulder and flank to get her to move forward. Then, before she could stop herself, she sneezed.

The mare scooted through the door to escape the cruel blows. The groom hung onto the lead shank and pulled her up sharply outside the stall. Then he looked up, searching the rafters. Christina knew he'd heard her sneeze.

She froze, leaning back against the joist, hoping he wouldn't see her. She still had a view of the man's dark face with his mean little eyes, and she realized that he could probably see her as well. Never taking his eyes off Christina, he smacked the mare hard in the shoulder again. When he did it, Christina jerked as if it were she who'd been hit. She felt her eyes well up with tears of sympathy for the abused horse. Then, still staring at her, the groom slowly raised his stick and extended it until it was pointing directly at Christina. There was no way she could misunderstand the threat.

The groom went off with the mare, and Christina

felt the tears begin to stream down her face. She had never felt so much hatred for a person and so much love for a horse. And never, in the whole twelve years of her life, had she ever felt so useless.

She made her way slowly back across the beam, until she was back over the wall of Matilda's stall. Matilda had been cooled out, bathed, and put back into her stall. And she was standing right underneath the place where Christina needed to climb down.

"Matilda, move over just a little, please," Christina begged her. The pretty black filly looked curiously at Christina, but she didn't move. At last Christina began climbing down anyway, which was much trickier than climbing up had been. Matilda was still in the way, so Christina ended up climbing onto the mare's back for a moment and then dismounting to get to the ground.

"Thanks, Tillie," Christina said, giving the filly a quick pat. Then she ducked under the stall guard and headed outside to find the racecourse. She had to see the gray mare run.

10

THE FIRST RACES AT BELMONT STARTED AT ONE O'CLOCK. Christina found her way to the paddock on the back side of the stands. Some horses were already standing tacked in the saddling stalls. Others were still being saddled by the jockeys' valets. Still others were being led around the oval walking ring in front of the saddling stalls. Christina didn't see the gray mare there yet. She found a spot where she had a good view of the horses as they entered the paddock area, and waited.

Soon she heard a ruckus and saw the groom leading the gray mare toward the paddock gate. Like the other horses, the mare's back legs were bandaged with "run downs" to protect against injury during the race. But unlike the other horses, who, though sometimes skittish, were always willing, the mare dragged her heels and balked all the way to the paddock gate. Christina saw that the groom was sweating with the effort of keeping the mare moving.

At the gate, the groom was handed a number to clip onto the horse's bridle. Christina knew that would indicate the mare's position in the starting gate. She saw that the number was three, third from the rail.

Then an official carrying a clipboard came to check the horse's tattoo. "Name?" he asked, flipping through the papers on his clipboard. Christina's ears perked up as she strained to hear the horse's name. "Sterling Dream," the groom said, pronouncing the words carefully.

"Sterling Dream," Christina repeated, whispering the name to herself. It was perfect.

The groom held Sterling's head tightly, jerking the chain shank across her nose if she so much as twitched a muscle, while the official examined the numbers tattooed on the inside of the mare's upper lip. Christina saw the whites of the mare's eyes and saw her trembling with anxiety. When the official released her lip, Sterling snapped at the groom, but he was ready for her. He jerked the chain severely across her nose and she flung her head up in pain.

The official raised an eyebrow but said nothing. He moved on to check the next horse entering the paddock. Christina had seen enough. She scurried out of the paddock and went into the grandstand.

She showed the man at the gate her pass and he

let her in, but her dusty blue jeans earned her a disapproving look. She realized everyone else was dressed up for the races and she quickly stuffed her shirttail into her jeans and tried to smooth her hair.

She wormed her way through the crowds of well-dressed spectators and came into the stands overlooking the racecourse. For a moment she hesitated, trying to pick out the best place to get a good view of the race. The mile-and-a-half dirt track sprawled before her, with its two inner turf courses and the infield the size of several football fields as perfectly groomed as a golf course.

"Hey, there," a friendly voice said. "I wondered if I'd see you here today. You looking for somebody?"

The voice was vaguely familiar. Christina saw a blond woman wearing khaki trousers and a blue sweater. She tried to think where she'd seen the woman before, then realized it was the carriage driver, Leanne.

"Hi, Leanne," Christina said, relieved to see a friendly face. "What are you doing here?"

"I told you, my Uncle Billy works here, and his horse, Studly, is running in the third race today. I practically grew up here, and I still like to come out once in a while for the races." She gestured to the overcast sky. "It's a terrible day to be driving a carriage in the city, but they race no matter what the weather. Where are your folks?"

Christina admitted that she was alone. She debated whether to tell Leanne about Sterling Dream.

"I came to see this one horse run," she finally said. "But I don't know where to sit."

"You don't want to sit," Leanne said. "You want to stand. Come with me." Christina followed her past rows and rows of seats, until they came to an enclosed area right in front of the finish wire. Leanne spoke to the guard at the gate as if they were old friends, and he unclipped the chain and let them through. "Here's the best place to see it up close," Leanne told her, leading her right up to the fence surrounding the outside rail of the track.

It wasn't the same as the view from the stands, but Christina realized that Leanne was right. She would be able to see the horses up close as they came down the stretch to the finish. Christina stood by the fence and listened to Leanne chatting while she waited anxiously for the race to start.

Soon the horses paraded by with their pony riders. The "ponies" were really just quiet horses who accompanied the Thoroughbreds in the post parade to keep them calm. Some of the Thoroughbreds just walked along quietly with their pony companions, while others were prancing and even cantering in their excitement as they entered the track. Some of the jockeys let their horses gallop a little to warm up, and others just walked or jogged to the starting gate. Christina got a good look at Sterling Dream as she came onto the track.

The horse looked uneasy. She kept tossing her

head as she jogged along beside her pony rider. The jockey wore red-and-white silks. Christina tugged on Leanne's sleeve. "That's the one," she said, pointing to Sterling. "That's the horse I like."

Leanne consulted her program. "Sterling Dream," she read. "Nice horse, but I don't think she's ever finished in the money. I know the owner. His name's Jimmy Furino. He's a nice guy, but he hasn't had too much success with his horses. This mare's his last hope, I think. I sure hope she wins."

Christina hoped Sterling Dream would win, too. Maybe then the groom wouldn't be so hard on her. "Who's the jockey?" Christina asked.

"I don't recognize him," Leanne said. "Let's see . . . Here it is. Terry McKenzie. Never heard of him," she said.

"What kind of race is this?" Christina asked.

"This is a maiden race for three-year-olds and up," Leanne told her. "You know what that means?"

Christina nodded. She knew that a maiden race was for horses who had never won a race before.

They were loading the horses into the starting gate. The first two went in without too much fuss. Christina watched anxiously as Sterling's turn came. The mare looked for a moment as though she was going to walk right in. Then suddenly she reared, scattering her handlers. The jockey came off. Furious, he leapt to his feet and smacked the horse across the rump with his whip.

"Oh, no!" Christina cried. "Why's he doing that?"

Leanne shook her head, looking disgusted. The handlers got the horse to stand still and put the jockey back on. This time Sterling went into the gate and stood. It seemed like an eternity to Christina, but really it was only a couple of minutes more before the start bell jangled and the announcer proclaimed, "They're off!"

Immediately the horses got down to the sport of running a race, and the crowds began the intense business of watching. Some people jumped up and down, shouting out the name of their favorite horse. Others clutched their programs in tense fists, chanting quietly as if it would help their horse run. Christina leaned over the fence as far as she could, straining to see Sterling. At last she caught a glimpse of Terry McKenzie's red-and-white silks flashing around the outside on the turn. The track was slick and muddy. Sterling Dream was running dead last, with gobs of mud splattering her face. The jockey was laying on the whip with every stride. There was a look of grim hatred on the mare's face, but she responded to the whip and began gaining ground.

Christina's heart sank. "She's not doing very well, is she?" she asked anxiously.

"She doesn't seem to be running well in the mud," Leanne said. "But maybe she likes to come from behind."

Sterling Dream was steadily gaining on the field.

She had passed several horses in the turn and was now in fifth. Christina had both fingers crossed as the horses rounded the turn and headed down the homestretch. "Go, Sterling!" Christina shouted, unable to resist being caught up in the excitement. "Go, go, go!"

Sterling had moved up to fourth. She was a dark silver streak as she slogged through the mud down the stretch toward the wire. "She's going to do it!" Christina shrieked. "She's going to win!"

Only two horses were ahead of her now, but they were neck and neck, blocking her path. Both jockeys were whipping the horses. Christina saw Sterling's ears flicker, and she seemed to hesitate. At the same moment, the inside horse moved off the rail, leaving an opening. Christina knew if Sterling could get through the opening, she could win, if only she had anything left in her. Terry began whipping her again, and Christina saw the mare's expression turn to fear. Sterling Dream put on a burst of speed and moved through the opening, passing the lead horse. Then, just three lengths before the finish, she veered to the left, and instead of crossing the wire, jumped over the inside rail and onto the turf course as the two other horses thundered under the wire, followed by the rest of the field.

Christina gasped and clutched Leanne's arm. "Look! Leanne, what's he doing? He's riding her onto the turf course."

Leanne shook her head. "I don't think the jockey did it. I think the horse did," she said.

The jockey had managed to stay on when the mare jumped over the inside rail, but he couldn't seem to stop her. Christina saw Sterling head for the turn, but instead of rounding it, she jumped the rail back onto the dirt track, dumping her jockey for the second time that day. Then she jumped over the outside rail. Christina had one last glimpse of Sterling jogging toward the back side of Belmont. But even after she lost sight of her, an image stayed in Christina's head. Over and over she saw the beautiful mare tucking her front legs and rounding her back as she jumped with perfect form over the rail. "That's the horse," Christina murmured. "That's the horse of my dreams."

That night at dinner Christina told her parents how she'd seen Sterling's groom abuse her. "He was so rough," Christina said indignantly. "And it was for no reason. She's not vicious at all—I'm sure of it. She's just afraid of him." Christina's dinner was growing cold before her. She was too worried to eat.

Her mother listened, frowning.

Her father put down his fork. "I told you to stay away from that horse," her father said sternly. "And I meant it. Don't you go near her or that side of the barn again."

"But, Dad, you said if I actually saw the groom do something, it would be different. This time I saw him! He beat her with a big stick." Christina held out her hands to show the length of it. She decided not to tell them about the groom's unspoken threat when he'd pointed the stick at her. "Can't we do something?"

"Christina, when I was your age I'm sure I would have felt the same way, so don't think I don't know how you feel," Ashleigh said. "But you've got to understand, there are a million different horses and a million different ways of handling them. You may not like the idea of it, but some horses need tough handlers. This mare you're talking about sounds vicious."

"That's what I told her, Ash," Mike commented. "From what I've heard, the mare's a biter and a kicker."

"I want to buy her," Christina suddenly announced. "I want an Event horse of my own, and I think Sterling is the one. I only have about a thousand dollars in my savings account, so I'll have to borrow the money from you guys. But I'll pay you back, I promise," Christina said quickly. She saw an amused twinkle in her father's eye and scowled. She wasn't kidding. Why didn't they ever take her seriously?

"Christina, even if she were for sale, which she may not be, she's a racehorse," her mother protested. "You're talking about completely retraining a horse who only knows one thing—how to run. It's much

143

more complicated than you think. Besides, Thoroughbreds are bred for speed. There's no guarantee that the mare can jump," Ashleigh pointed out. "You're assuming a lot of things about this horse and you've never even ridden her."

"She can too jump," Christina said. Then she told them about the race—how Sterling had come from behind and then jumped off the track.

"I bet the owner wasn't too pleased with that," Mike commented. "Wait 'til you see Legacy run on Wednesday. You'll be a happy owner, I bet."

Christina groaned. "I would be happy to be the owner of an Event horse!" she wailed, dropping her forehead on her folded arms.

Mike glanced at his watch and signaled the waiter to bring the check. "We should get going. We only have half an hour before the show starts."

They went to a Broadway show, but Christina was too distracted to enjoy it. She couldn't stop thinking about Sterling Dream. How could she convince her parents to buy the horse? Again and again she imagined the horse jumping, but this time she was riding her. They were galloping down a hillside toward a water jump. Then they were sailing over it, flawlessly, effortlessly, endlessly.

"Chrissy? Chris."

Someone was shaking her shoulder. Christina opened her eyes and saw that it was her father. The show was over. She had fallen asleep in her seat.

• • •

Monday and Tuesday there were no races at Belmont. The family spent all day Monday shopping and sight-seeing. On Tuesday, Christina persuaded her parents to take her back to Belmont instead of taking her to the Metropolitan Museum of Art. She convinced them that she wanted to watch Legacy's training now that race day was approaching, but the truth was, she just wanted to see Sterling Dream again.

Christina had just come from watching Legacy's workout on Tuesday morning. She was walking back to the barn with Anna Simms, who was going to be Legacy's jockey in his first race on Wednesday. Anna was still an apprentice jockey, but she had already ridden in a few races. Since Legacy was used to her, Ashleigh had decided to let Anna ride the horse.

"Your mom is the greatest, Christina," Anna bubbled. "Not many people would give a bug like me a chance to ride such a great horse," she said appreciatively.

Christina was only half listening to Anna. "Did you see a pretty dapple-gray mare when you were out there with Legacy?" she asked Anna. She couldn't keep her mind off of Sterling Dream. She was worried that the mare hadn't been there.

Anna shook her head and went on raving about Legacy. "It's going to be a great race for him—I can feel it," Anna said enthusiastically. "He's never been more ready."

145

"Mm-hmm," Christina agreed absently. She wanted her horse to win, but right now she was more concerned with trying to figure out how she could check on Sterling Dream without getting herself in trouble.

Just as they reached the barn, Christina glimpsed a dapple-gray hindquarter vanishing behind another barn. She was sure it was Sterling. "Excuse me, Anna," she said, and hurried across the lane and around the side of the building where she'd seen the horse.

It was Sterling. There was a turnout paddock there, and the groom was leading Sterling to it. As usual, she was fighting him all the way. Christina hung back, watching. The groom led the horse into the paddock and unclipped the lead shank. He had to scoot quickly out of the way, dodging two metal-shod hooves as Sterling wheeled around quick as a flash and kicked at him with both hind legs before galloping off. Christina almost laughed out loud. She half wished the mare had actually gotten him.

The groom studied the horse, who ran around the paddock, faster and faster. She snorted in defiance at the hated groom as she flashed past. Christina thought she would surely stumble in the little circle, but she never missed a step. "Why you no run on the racetrack like you run in here?" he said angrily.

As if in reply, the mare kicked up her heels, twisting them toward the groom as she tore by.

Christina gasped as Sterling narrowly missed kicking him in the head.

"Witch! I make you sorry you did that," the man said. He shook his head, scowling, and stalked away with the lead shank, leaving the mare to run free. Christina waited until he was out of sight, then came out from the shadow of the building and walked slowly toward the paddock.

Sterling Dream's head was turned toward where the groom had gone. Her angry gallop slowed and she broke into a trot. Then she stopped, flanks heaving, head and tail raised in defiance. When she was satisfied that the man was gone, she finally relaxed. She dropped her nose toward the sand and walked around, nosing at the footing until she found just the right spot. She gave a sigh and sunk down on her side in the soft sand. Then she turned belly-up and rolled, letting the soft, scratchy sand massage her back. Christina watched, enjoying seeing the mare look happy for a change. Sterling rolled all the way over, wriggled happily on the other side, then stood up. She let out several enormous snorts, clearing the dust from her nostrils, then shook herself vigorously all over. Christina could have sworn she was shaking off the bad feelings the groom gave her.

Then Sterling noticed Christina. For a moment the mare's ears went back in fear. Then she must have realized that Christina wouldn't hurt her. She stepped confidently forward.

Christina let the horse make the first move. She stood still and let the mare nuzzle her hair. Not for one moment did she feel that the horse would bite or kick her. Christina was positive that Sterling was only vicious when the groom was around.

Sterling began to trot around the little ring. She kept her eye on Christina as she threw her slender front legs before her in a beautifully smooth extension. The mare nearly floated, her perfect neck arched, her neat black hooves hardly touching the ground. She seemed to be showing off for Christina, who watched delightedly.

"Is this the horse?"

Christina turned and saw her mother. She nodded, beaming happily. "Isn't she gorgeous? Just look at that extended trot."

Ashleigh and Christina watched as the mare stopped, spun on her haunch, and began to canter gracefully in the other direction. Christina sighed. She had never wanted something so badly in her life. And it didn't look as if she would ever be able to have it.

11

WEDNESDAY MORNING THE REESES ATE BREAKFAST AT THE hotel, then headed for the track. In honor of Legacy's big day, Mike had hired a limousine to take them to Belmont. Christina pretended not to care, but actually it was pretty cool. She had never ridden in a limo before.

Wonder's Legacy was set to run in the third race of the day. Before they went to the track, the Reeses went by the barn to check on the horses and make sure everything was going smoothly. Christina peeked into Legacy's stall, where Anna was wrapping his hind legs in run downs. The horse looked handsome and fit, and completely up to the importance of the occasion.

Seated in their box in the grandstand, Christina began to feel the excitement in the air. Katie had been right, Christina thought. It was going to be thrilling watching her own horse run.

Soon she spotted Wonder's Legacy in the post parade, escorted by Naomi on one of the ponies. "Look—there he is!" she said to her parents. Christina eyed her colt, comparing him to the other horses. She had to admit he was splendid-looking.

"It's a whole other picture from up here, isn't it?" her mother said, smiling. "How does it feel to be the owner of that fine-looking colt?"

"It feels pretty good," Christina admitted, watching Legacy proceed toward the gate. Anna let Legacy gallop a little to take the edge off, but the big colt looked calm and happy.

A man about her father's age, with a pleasant face and auburn hair under a "Breeder's Cup" cap, was looking curiously at her. "Is that your colt?" he asked her. "Number seven?"

"That's my colt," Christina said proudly. "His name's Wonder's Legacy. He's a two-year-old and this is his first race."

"Good luck to you," the man said. "That's a classy-looking animal you got there. If only looks were enough." Then he sighed deeply. "If there's one thing I've learned in all my years in the business, it's that there's no such thing as a sure thing. I got a horse right now that I put the last of my money into. She's got great breeding, great looks, she's fast as anything, but the horse just doesn't want to run." He shook his head. "The other day I ran her and she had the race in the bag, and you know what she did?"

Christina shook her head. She was only half listening to the man as she watched Legacy approach the gate.

"Three lengths from the wire, she jumped off the track and onto the turf course. That race was supposed to be my big win and it turned out to be nothing but a big laugh," he continued.

Jumped off the track? The start bell hadn't sounded yet, but Christina jumped as if it had. She turned to the man. "What's your horse's name?" she asked him.

"Sterling Dream," he said.

"Oh!" Christina exclaimed. "You must be Mr. Furino. I know your horse. She's beautiful," Christina said.

The man looked puzzled. "How do you know me?"

"We're in the same barn as you, on the other side," Christina explained.

"Well, then you do know my horse. Her name ought to be Sterling Nightmare after that race," he joked. "In fact, that race pretty much convinced me it's time to get out of the horse business. Never made a dime in ten years. I'm getting rid of my last two horses and calling it quits."

"Jim Furino!" A man a couple of seats down was calling and waving.

"Bill Dodson!" Mr. Furino called back. To

Christina he said, "Excuse me just a minute." He began talking to the other man.

"Mom! Dad!" Christina said urgently. "That's Sterling Dream's owner, sitting right next to me! And he says he's getting out of the horse business and that Sterling is for sale! Can't we buy her, please?" Christina pleaded.

"I saw the horse, Mike," her mother said. "She's a gorgeous mover, and her legs looked good to me. Christina says she saw her jump."

"I guess we could offer him seven or eight thousand and see what he says," her father said. Her parents locked eyes. Christina saw her mother nod slightly.

"Yes!" Christina whispered joyously, clasping her hands together.

"Look—Legacy's loading into the gate," Ashleigh said, directing Christina's attention back to the race. Legacy had the number seven post position in the field of twelve horses. He went easily into the gate and stood while the last five horses were loaded after him. Then the start bell rang. "Theeey're off!" the announcer chanted.

Christina dutifully watched Legacy's race, but all she could think about was that Sterling would soon be hers.

"He broke from the gate a little slow," Ashleigh said anxiously.

Christina watched the horses moving down the

back side toward the turn. She spotted Anna's blue-and-white silks and saw that they were stuck behind a pack of three horses.

"Come on, Anna. Find a hole," Ashleigh muttered, watching intently. Christina saw Legacy creep forward and suddenly he was past the three horses and gaining ground quickly.

"Go, go, go!" Ashleigh chanted.

Wonder's Legacy was still moving up as the pack thundered down the homestretch to the wire. Legacy came in third. It was all over in less than a minute, but to Christina it seemed to take hours.

"Well, he ran a good race," Ashleigh remarked.

"If he hadn't gotten boxed in back there before the turn, he'd have won it," Mike said. "Don't worry, Chris." He put an arm around his daughter. "He's a winner. He just needs a longer race, that's all."

"Mike," Ashleigh said softly, flashing a smile at Christina. "I don't think Chris is thinking about Legacy's race right now. Let's see if we can find out about the horse she wants."

As if on cue, Mr. Furino approached the Reeses. "Congratulations," he said to Christina. "Your horse did well for his first time out there. I wish my horse had half your horse's heart."

She does, Christina wanted to say. Instead she said, "Mr. Furino, these are my parents."

Mike introduced himself and Ashleigh. "We heard you might be interested in selling your mare," Mike began. "We've been looking for a horse for my daughter, and she—we—feel that your mare might be a good choice for her."

Christina felt her heart flop with excitement. It was really going to happen!

Mr. Furino hesitated. Then he said, "Well, to tell you the truth, this mare's kind of a problem. She's a biter and a kicker, and she hasn't run well. She's kind of got a screw loose, if you know what I mean."

"You'd bite, too, if someone beat you all the time," Christina muttered.

"What'd you say?" Mr. Furino asked.

Mike gave Christina a warning look that made her close her mouth. "I'm prepared to give you eight thousand for the horse," Mike offered.

"Sorry," Mr. Furino replied, shaking his head. "But this is no kid's horse. You've seen how she is. Anyway, like I said, I've had it with racehorses. Never made me a dime. The next race is a claiming race. I've entered Sterling in it and hopefully somebody'll claim her and that'll be the end of it. If not, at least maybe I can win back some of the money I've put into training the horse until someone does claim her. Sorry, kid," he said sincerely to Christina.

At first Christina was completely dejected. Then she realized that if Sterling Dream was entered in a claiming race, anyone could file a claim on the horse for whatever the set amount was, and after the race, the horse could be claimed. "Dad!" Christina nearly shouted. "We can claim Sterling!"

"Do we have time?" Mike asked.

"I think we can file a claim up to ten minutes before the race starts," Ashleigh confirmed.

"Well, let's go!" Christina nearly shouted.

At the claims desk, Mike began filling out the forms.

"Be sure you spell her name right," Ashleigh warned him. "If you don't, the claim is invalid."

"It's S-t-e—" Christina began.

"I know how to spell it, sweetheart," her father said good-naturedly.

When the claim had been officially filed, Ashleigh left to check on Anna and Wonder's Legacy. She promised to meet Christina and Mike at the detention barn when Sterling's race was over. Christina nearly dragged her father back to their seats. The horses were being loaded into the gate already. Sterling had the number nine post position, furthest from the rail. Christina held her breath as Sterling fought her handlers going into the gate. At last she was loaded and the bell rang.

"Oh, I can't watch," Christina moaned, covering her eyes. As soon as the race was over, the horse would be hers. But what if something happened to Sterling in the race? What if she tried jumping off the track again and injured herself somehow?

But then, of course, she had to watch. Christina

opened her eyes and saw that Sterling was moving up from behind as she had before, a look of intense hatred on her gray face as the jockey whipped her past horse after horse. Christina flinched with every stroke of the whip. "Soon you'll be mine," she whispered, "and you won't have to do this ever again."

At last the horses crossed the finish wire, Sterling in fifth place. Christina saw the jockey begin slowing the mare, a disgusted look on his face. But she hardly noticed. "Come on, Dad," she said, tugging on his hand.

Mike stood up. "Okay. Let's go get your horse," he said.

Christina's heart was racing with anticipation. Could this really be happening? It was all Christina could do to keep from skipping as they entered the detention barn. Mike steered her toward the claims officials standing nearby. He was just about to ask about Sterling when suddenly there was a scuffle and what sounded like shouts of distress coming from one of the stalls.

"What the heck is that?" Mike asked.

Then the shouts grew louder. Someone was really in trouble. Suddenly Christina recognized the shouts. With a chill she realized that Sterling's groom was in the stall with the horse. That was where the disturbance was coming from.

"Oh, no," Christina cried. Had the groom finally

really hurt the horse? She ran down the shedrow and peered into the stall, dreading what she might see.

The groom was indeed in the stall with Sterling Dream. The horse was leaning against him, pinning him against the stall wall with her powerful haunches. The groom was in a panic, yelling and cursing, trying fruitlessly to push the mare away from him. She wasn't kicking, just holding him there. Christina saw a kind of grim resolution in the horse's face, as if she had decided that she just couldn't take it anymore, and she would hold her weight against the groom until one of them quit fighting.

By then several other people had come to see what the ruckus was about. Christina knew she'd better act fast. If anyone else tried to get to the mare, she might react by biting or kicking. Christina was hoping that the mare would remember her well enough to let her coax her away from the groom. She ducked into the stall before anyone could stop her.

"Hey!" came a shout from behind her. "Don't go in there. That mare's crazy. She'll kill you!"

Christina ignored the warning. The pinned groom saw her and started begging her to help him. "Be quiet," Christina admonished him. "You're just making it worse." The man lowered his voice, but he didn't stop talking.

The mare was wearing her halter and a lead shank was on the floor nearby. Christina guessed that the groom had been trying to catch her and had finally bullied her to the breaking point. Christina thought it was about time. She picked up the lead shank and came slowly toward the mare's head, talking in a soft, kind voice.

"Christina, get out of there before you get kicked," her father called. "I'll get the horse."

"No, Dad!" Christina said in a voice that was both quiet and sharp. The mare kicked back viciously with one hind leg. "Just let me do it," Christina said calmly.

She slowly reached out and put a gentle hand on Sterling's neck, feeling the mare quiver at her touch. Sterling's muscles were bunched with fear and tension under the gray satin coat. Christina continued talking to the terrified horse, stroking her over and over as the gray ears flipped back and forth between Christina and the groom she still held pinned against the wall. Finally the mare responded to Christina's caring touch. She shifted her haunches and released the groom.

Christina had intended to clip the lead shank on and lead the mare away, but she hadn't counted on the groom's reaction. The second he felt the mare relax her weight slightly, he wriggled frantically out from behind her, scaring the mare again.

"No!" Christina said urgently. "Be still!"

But it was too late. The mare kicked at the groom and caught him squarely in the gut. He moaned and fell to the stall floor, clutching his stomach. Christina made one deft reach with the clip and managed to hook the lead shank onto the halter. The mare cowered behind Christina, as if she thought Christina could protect her. "Don't worry," Christina told her. "Nothing will happen to you, I promise. They can't blame you for that." But Christina was sick with worry. What if the groom was really hurt? What would they do to Sterling?

Sterling Dream followed Christina docilely out of the stall. Christina held the horse while several people went in to see if the fallen groom was going to be all right. A few moments later, he came out of the stall on his own two feet, helped by two other guys. He was pasty-faced, still clutching his stomach, but he looked as if he was going to recover.

"Chris, are you okay?" Her father rushed to her side.

"I'm fine, Dad," she assured him. "Can we take Sterling out of here now?" she asked. "I think she's had enough of this place." Christina glared meaning-fully at the groom.

"You're a great little handler," Mr. Furino said to Christina. He had come in time to see her get Sterling away from the groom.

"Thanks," Christina said. "She's just sensitive."

"Sensitive my eye," Mr. Furino said. "That horse is just bad news. She's no horse for a kid. Why don't you let me hold her before she starts acting up again?"

"She's not bad!" Christina protested. "She just doesn't trust that groom," Christina said, pointing to the man. He was sitting on a bale of hay, still looking a little nauseous. "You wouldn't either if he beat you all the time," Christina courageously said.

"Christina," Mike protested.

"What do you mean?" Mr. Furino asked.

Christina took a deep breath. She figured she might as well tell him everything. With all the grown-ups around, she didn't have to fear the groom. "I mean," Christina said, "your groom abuses this horse. I saw him do it." Christina described the beatings she had witnessed.

"You lie!" the groom protested angrily. Now his face was red instead of white. "This girl lie! I no hit the horse. That horse, she crazy. She kick me! She bite me! She try to kill me!"

"No, you're lying," Christina said levelly. She had spotted something in the straw just inside the mare's stall. "Dad, look." Christina pointed. Half buried in the stall where the groom had dropped it was the fat stick he'd used to beat Sterling. Mike went over and picked it up. "That's the stick I told you about," Christina declared.

Everyone stared at the groom, who spluttered and protested that he'd never seen the stick before. Then he stood up. "You watch. I no hurt the horse." He stepped toward Sterling. The mare instantly pinned her ears, baring her teeth in warning.

"Stop!" Christina said, holding the mare steady. "You stay away from her. You've scared her enough already."

Jim Furino eyed the groom. "You know something? I've never liked you. I just kept you on because my trainer said you were good. But I'm through with horses, so I don't have to listen to him anymore. You're fired," he said to the groom. "You can get out of here right now."

"Now, Jim, wait just a minute," a seedy-looking red-haired fellow said. Christina supposed he must be the trainer. "We need to discuss this before you go off and—"

"And you." Mr. Furino cut him off. "You've been telling me for five years that we just need to discuss things a little more. I'm tired of your discussion. I've poured money and horses down the drain for ten years. This mare was my last try. She's got the bloodlines on both sides. She's got the speed. And she's got class. If you were any kind of a trainer, you'd have produced something by now. I'm through with the horses, and I'm through with you."

"Now, Jim—"

"Take him, and get out of here," Mr. Furino said coldly.

The groom glared at Mr. Furino, at Christina, at the other people who had gathered. He spat angrily into the dirt, then stomped off. The trainer looked bitterly around him, then reluctantly followed the groom out of the barn. For a moment, there was silence. Then slowly, a few people began to applaud.

Mr. Furino raised an eyebrow. "I guess those guys were even less popular than I realized," he said.

A pretty, well-dressed woman with dark hair approached. Christina hadn't seen her before. "I'll take her now," she said warmly, putting out a hand toward Sterling's lead shank.

Christina was puzzled. Was the woman a claims official? She wasn't wearing a badge.

"No, I'll stay with her. She's still kind of upset." Christina put a protective arm over the mare's withers.

"Who are you?" the woman said.

"Who are you?" Mike asked her, putting an arm around Christina.

"I'm Ellen Cargan," the woman said. Then she gestured to Sterling. "This is my horse."

12

CHRISTINA LOOKED FROM THE WOMAN TO HER DAD, WIDE-eyed, feeling panic rising inside her. "There must be some mistake," she protested. "Sterling's mine. We claimed her, right, Dad?" She looked desperately at her father for reassurance, but what she found in his blue eyes was sadness.

"I'm sorry, Chrissy," he said gently. "It looks like someone else has claimed your horse."

"How can that be?" Christina said. She whirled to face the woman. "What are you talking about, Dad?" Christina said. "Sterling is mine. We claimed her."

The woman looked uncomfortable. "I'm afraid I claimed her, too. I guess that means we have to shake for her."

Shake? What did she mean? Christina stared uncomprehendingly at her father.

163

"Sometimes it happens, Chris," he explained. "When more than one person claims a horse, they have to draw to see who gets the claim."

"That's right," the claiming official said. "I have both your claims here." He showed them the two claiming slips. "When more than one person claims a horse, and the claims are all valid, we put a number for each person in a bottle, shake it up, and draw one. Whoever's number we draw becomes the new owner. It's the only fair way to settle it," he said with an apologetic look at Christina.

Christina thought she might actually throw up. She had come so close to owning Sterling and now she might lose her again. Suddenly Christina wanted her mother.

As if she'd known, Ashleigh appeared by her side. "Mom!" Christina said. "Something terrible is happening."

"What is it?" Ashleigh asked, putting an arm around Christina's shoulders.

Mike explained the situation and Ashleigh sighed. "Well, let's get this over with," she said.

The claims official nodded. He showed them number one, Ms. Cargan's number, and number two for Christina, and then dropped the numbers into a container. He shook them up for a few seconds.

"Two, two, two," Christina whispered tensely. Then the second official reached in and drew a number. Christina could hardly breathe. The official looked at the number in his hand. Then he looked at Christina and smiled a small, tight-lipped smile. Christina almost smiled back. Was it her number?

"Number one," the claims official said. "Ms. Cargan, you're the owner." He showed the number to everyone.

Christina felt the back of her eyes begin to sting. She lowered her head, letting her hair fall across her cheeks where it would hide her tears. They began to splash upon her shoes, and all she could do was watch them fall. She hadn't known a person's heart could actually ache, but hers did. She had lost Sterling and she felt as though she would never, ever be happy again.

"I'll take her now," Ms. Cargan said gently.

Slowly, sadly, Christina handed over the lead shank, and with it, her dream. She would never find another horse like Sterling.

"Wait," Mike said. "Ms. Cargan, we're prepared to offer you the claiming price, plus another twenty-five hundred for the horse," he said.

Ms. Cargan hesitated. "I understand how you feel," she said. "But I've had my eye on this horse for several months now. I've just been waiting for her to run in a claiming race so I could get her. It's the horse that's important to me, not the money," she explained. "I'm really sorry, Christina."

Suddenly Christina had an idea. She swiped at her eyes and looked at Ms. Cargan levelly. "I would like to make you an offer," she said. "I'll trade you my horse, Wonder's Legacy, for Sterling."

"Christina," her father protested. "Wonder's Legacy is worth—"

"Dad," Christina cut him off. "Remember when you bought Faith, and everyone laughed at you, but you just had a feeling about her and you said that sometimes you just had to follow your heart and take a leap of faith?" She paused. All the adults were looking at her. "Well, this is my leap of faith," she said softly. "I know there's something about Sterling that I'll never find in another horse. I know she's meant to be with me. So I'd like to offer you my horse for Sterling," she said again to Ms. Cargan.

"Oh, Christina, I don't know . . . ," Ms. Cargan said doubtfully.

"He's a good horse. He's worth five times what you paid for Sterling," Christina said.

"Christina, you can't—" Mike started to say.

"Let her do it, Mike," Ashleigh said quietly.

Christina's eyes met her mother's and they shared a moment of complete understanding.

"It's time you got the horse you really wanted," Ashleigh said quietly to her. "I'm sorry I didn't realize sooner."

When Ms. Cargan agreed, Christina's heart lifted

as if it had wings and would soar right out of her chest. She threw her arms around her mother and held on to her tightly, unable to believe all that had happened in the past few days.

A few days later she was finally cantering her own horse, Sterling Dream, across a lush pasture back home at Whitebrook Farm. Kevin was cantering along beside her on Jasper, but this time they weren't racing—they were just riding. A few moments later Christina spied the fallen tree. She brought Sterling to a walk, and Kevin made Jasper walk beside her.

Christina and Kevin eyed the tree. "Go ahead," Kevin said, pulling up.

Christina looked out across the pasture and spotted her mother standing in the backyard watching her. She waved and her mother waved back. Christina gathered up the reins, and when she asked, Sterling made a perfect transition to a canter. She cantered up to the tree, and when the mare jumped, it was exactly as Christina had dreamed it would be. With perfect form they soared over it, flawlessly, endlessly, effortlessly, and it was better than Trib's best round, better than the three-six oxer with Foster, better than anything. Christina patted Sterling's shining neck as she brought her to a walk. In a little while, Katie Garrity and Dylan Becker would be coming over to tell her about the Event at

Foxwood and to check out her new horse. As Christina turned and cantered toward the fallen tree again, she didn't think she could possibly be any happier.